To MS [...]

THANK you so Much!

Pleasant Dreams

Ferris Shelton
2019

Seven Full Days

By Ferris Shelton

An Off the Common Book, Amherst, Massachusetts

Printed in the United States of America

ISBN: 978-1-945473-70-8

Acknowledgements
Every one critically important:

1st and Foremost, my Higher Power

Rochelle O'Gorman

Cambridge College

Northampton Veterans Administration Medical Center

Dr. Katherine Putnam, PHD

Jerry Bronaugh

OmoWunmi Shelton

Howard Caswell

Venessa Cline

Quality Grain

Harriet 'Nana Esi' Cornelius

Steven Quarshie

Carla Byers

Richard Keefe

Rayvon K. Shelton

Jamaica Plains Veterans Administration

Brockton Veterans Administration

The United States Marine Corps

Lizbeth Glickman

Callie Nelson

Heike Barthel

Jermail Shelton

Shafon Scott

Laraeh Shelton

Smith College

Merrilyn Lewis

Rhonda Skinner

Janice Mazzallo

J. R. Cotton

Monique Barnes

Kevin Baylor

Hyacinth Dixon

Sue Woods

Cynthia Woodley

Audrey Terrell

In Loving Memory of
Mae Shelton, 1935 to 2016

Contents

Prologue

A life altering change will remain still, quietly hibernating in a person for years. We often choose comfortable, well-established order over the disruption change can cause, thus it is seldom awakened. But a sleeping giant could animate if affected by the right forces. And, if it does, what was once safely tucked away in the out-of-sight, out-of-mind compartment of our psyche will extract a heavy toll - even if aroused by innocent intentions. Unbeknownst to Jason, this day would start a process of change that sat deep within, slumbering but ready to stir.

Sunday

The Trigger

Chapter 1

'Thank God,' Callie thought after seeing the first group of people exiting the front door. It was the first indication that this sorry-ass party was coming to an end. Having lost all ability to even fake interest in the gathering, she sat in a soft-leather chair, large and plush enough to curl up in - except her posture was of someone being grilled by an authority figure. These uncomfortable surroundings caused her to search for any reasonable excuse to make a graceful exit.

Another problem, that exit required her husband and he was nowhere to be seen as she sat in a vast, high-ceiling living room.

She was amongst a group of women talking the way women do when they really don't know each other well. There were seven altogether; six were guests, wives (including Callie), or girlfriends of company staff. The effort of this group of ladies was to pass time, as opposed to having a good time.

The seventh woman and party hostess was Mrs. Calhoun. Extreme facial wrinkles and a slight, bony frame made her look much older than her husband, even though they met as teenagers. The years had worn away any evidence of love, leaving him as prickly and dominant as she was demur and docile. She may as well have been the maid. If there ever was a classically repressed woman, Mrs. Calhoun was it. Lacking contemporary social skill, she painted on a dutiful smile.

She wore a confused look on her face, cocking her head toward anyone talking at the time, like an unsure pet looking for further instruction. She wore a long plain summer dress and sat in an armless, antique Lady's chair. Sitting erect, she presented the well-rehearsed mannerisms of blueblood upbringing. But Callie thought that this was not the audience for such phoniness.

In one of the two wooden-armed, French provincial chairs was the 'big talker.' She was the only woman whom Callie had even a passing acquaintance. Her name was Renae, and although she mostly dominated the conversation, without her motor mouth this sham of a party would be even worse.

The main discourse had become exclusive, involving the company women. The gist was personal, intra-office stuff. Far from interested, Callie tuned them out, but after seeing people exit that front door for the first time, she was primed for the opportunity to do the same. With that purpose in mind, Callie listened in to the conversation, hoping for a period of silence or for one of the other woman to announce they were leaving.

"When we talk to each other, he just be looking at me. If he in the room and I'm working close by, I can feel his eyes all over me. He stands all close and when I move he just be leaning against me. Yechhhh!" Renae said, flicking her fingers as if trying to remove something sticky from her nails. The corners of her mouth turned down, emphasizing her disgust.

"Shoots, girl you should say something," responded one of the other company women.

"Say what? He's just a harmless pest but I don't see how he could think I would want him. He old and looks soft as jelly. I mean, he really not my type."

"Well, has he said anything?"

"Oh, nothing out of line, he always careful not to come on too strong, even though he always brushing against me. Then he say, 'excuse me,' while looking down at what he just rubbed against. He has asked me out, as he say, 'for cocktails' after work. But, it's always to talk over some work assignment."

"Assignment! Girl you know what's being ass-signed."

Callie thought she would not be able to stand one more minute of this drivel; it had become entirely too familiar. Renae, the woman complaining this time, sat sipping wine in a tight, short skirt revealing much more thigh than the occasion called for. Her outfit looked to be a standing invitation for every male come-on.

This script and cast was redundant; same stuff, different day - the clacking class killing time discussing the mundane. She and Jason arrive at these functions together but often, after dinner, they settle into different rooms. He is brainwashed with foolishness someplace else while she endures talk of pecan pie recipes, weight-loss diets, and stylish shoe sales at the Lenox Mall. As boring as that usually was now they were swerving into specific Edwards's office goings-on and she was fed up.

Standing, she asked the hostess, "Your bathroom, is it down this hall or back through the kitchen?"

"It's right down the hall love, on the right," responded Mrs. Calhoun, waving her arm as if she were Vanna White pointing out a vowel.

After exiting the room, Callie looked for her husband. In this big house he could be in any of five rooms on this side of the front entrance or the ample space outside that included three separate landscaped gardens. Her irritation was not easily disguised as she stepped from one room to another. Callie found it better to walk on the balls of her feet. Her heels striking on the tiled foyer floor expressed her agitation much more than she intended.

Soon there would be a right time to put those all-to-real frustrations with her husband on display.

Callie went room to room, smiling whenever encountering another guest. While searching for Jason, she smoldered inside about how things needed to get better in their relationship. These social events were not fun for her, but he just didn't care. Recently other important issues she wanted to discuss were ending with him shutting down all avenues of communication by not being willing to consider that she had a worthwhile opinion. It was patronizing. It was condescending. And it was pissing her off.

A check of a third room and there he was, sitting at a table with the host and, as always, The Jackass. Slinking into the room cat-quiet, Callie snuggled close to Jason whispering softly, "Are you ready to go home, Jason?"

"Their knee grows!" exclaimed Bob Farrington. He sat at the table's corner reaching down with both hands to demonstrate his words by separating flattened inward facing palms setting out from his knee - one lowering toward the ankle the other rising toward the thigh. "Get it, 'why are African-Americans so tall?' - their knee grows, really!"

Erupting in laughter, Bob had not noticed Callie, even as Jason and Clay Calhoun nodded in her direction.

"Oh now Bob, you should be careful when there's mixed company around," chided Clay, the host of the affair, smiling at Callie.

"No need, Jason and I have moved beyond political-correctness," Farrington said before noticing Callie at Jason's side adding, "Oh, but I hadn't seen the lady join us. Hi, Callie what are the girls doing?"

"We just talkin'," Callie stated trying to hide the fact that she was disturbed and offended by the joke. Yet she was forced to assume the posture of the good wife in front of this rude man. Seething beneath the surface, she managed a half-hearted, obligatory smile designed to begin the process of getting them both out that front door.

"Jason, you know I have choir practice tomorrow," stated Callie calmly.

"Okay honey, we were just finishing up. Give me a minute to say goodbye."

That was exactly what she wanted to hear, a fact expressed with a firm pat on his knee along with a very agreeable exclamation, "I'll get my things." She walked away as Jason stood and extended his hand. Farrington grabbed the offering saying, "Sounds like taps my man."

Callie waited in the doorway as Jason said goodbye. She hated the way Jason acted in these settings, accepting indignities that were, in her opinion, unacceptable. She was seeing it more and more and it bothered her. Stepping aside as he approached the door, she glared a look of unmistakable displeasure. Walking past completely disconnected, he was so oblivious to everything regarding her these days that he didn't even notice.

Callie put back on her 'nice' face, grabbed his arm and together they made their way toward the front door, her heels staccato-like on the tile floor. Retrieving her purse while going through the polite motions of making the hostess actually believe she enjoyed the party, they finally left the house, and all pretense disappeared. By the time they arrived at the car, she was hot – reflecting that fact with a car-rocking slam of the passenger side door.

Chapter 2

It was late Sunday evening when they pulled out of the driveway of Clay Calhoun's dinner-party in Marietta, Georgia, an Atlanta suburb. The well-lit house, standing majestic, was located in an upper class gated community alongside other opulent three-story homes. Jason Scott, an African American man growing in confidence, considered himself perfectly positioned to one day live in a similar neighborhood.

He was driven by this craving for success. It colored every minute of his day, based on careful, self-nurtured behavior, seeded in childhood. With a fertile, impressionistic mind, he made character-shaping decisions early in life and perceived no need for subsequent adjustments. The result of this personal inertia was the man named Jason Scott.

His ambitious nature had turned into an obsession and was rarely decorated with other aspects of a fulfilling life unless Jason thought those other things directly contributed to that all-consuming focus. This desire had become a behemoth, ethically based and ruthlessly applied. Blessed with a Talented Tenth intellect that was encouraged and nurtured from childhood, he committed early to comprehending the best avenue for what he wanted. Never considering his chosen path lacked pragmatism.

Jason developed a self-important certitude that, for the most part was subconscious, but nevertheless was beginning to affect his personality and behavior. Every action associated with a business presentation was thought out, rehearsed and refined.

He wanted to be a shaker and a mover. Proud and cocksure, he had no reason to question this approach to his goals. And neither did anyone else.

Jason groomed himself for this perceived destiny, wearing a well-manicured mustache, goatee, and short-cropped hair that highlighted his good-boy looks. A large head, deep-chocolate unblemished skin and coffee-bean colored eyes looked masculine, rough but not rough-neck. Staying with an old style even as frame designs and shapes evolved over the years, he chose to wear wire-rimmed glasses solely for the purpose of looking smart.

For the past few years Callie encouraged him to try contacts or one of the new surgical procedures. Jason thought 'eye surgery' was not worth the risk, especially when it was not mandatory or, for that matter, even necessary. To him, contact lenses took away from his carefully cultivated appearance.

His broad shoulders and muscular tone augmented a wide gregarious smile, framed by full lips containing straight white teeth. It was the entire aesthetic package that contributed to his imposing, natural presence. He had a wide bridged nose that fit comfortably within the surrounding contours of a face containing evenly spaced, bright, lively eyes. A rich, baritone voice rounded out an impressive purpose-driven person.

Exiting the community gate, Jason drove away with Callie sitting quietly in the passenger seat. There was a cold chill expressed in their silence; a noticeable uneasiness in her after-party manner. Attempting to start-up a conversation recapping the party's general gossip, he talked alone. On this night, his usual chatterbox of a wife sat distant, obviously upset about something.

Not sure of exactly what, he quickly reviewed his actions at the informal gathering. Had he flirted with any of the women at the party? Had he been rude or mean to her, either privately or in front of others?

Callie Scott, a red-bone beauty of a woman was feminine through and through. Her slender frame delicately contained a wiry body and, having jumped double-dutch well into her teens, it sat atop fleshy, well-shaped *'Dancers' Legs.'* At five-foot ten, her posture was tall and elegant. With a friendly presentation and a welcoming demeanor, people warmed to her quickly. She was not viewed as a threat, even among women competing to be the center of attention.

Callie could be passionate about certain issues without giving a damn about what others thought. And as Jason knew all too well, with personal or family matters, she could wear her emotions openly. One had to be close to her to see this side, for her upbringing was steeped in Southern hospitality. She held tight to traditions associated with a good church girl.

She was the youngest child of a large family that included four brothers, three sisters and countless aunts, uncles and cousins. Her situation was such that she had a couple of nieces and nephews older than her. The youngest by seven years, Callie grew up showered with the attention afforded the baby of a large family - and not just from Mom, Dad and siblings.

She had always been told she was special and by the time she became an adult, she came to believe it. Being confident that someone would always protect her, she was outspoken as a child, but not in a selfish, brat-like way. She championed the girls spending as much time out of the house, and thus having equal freedom with the boys, although through her late teen years and into young adulthood she preferred to stay close to home.

She could sit with Dad after a hard day's work and help Mom in the kitchen. She loved them both equally and showed it. Innately harboring a soft toughness with strong compassion, these seemingly competing traits coexisted in her character, nurturing a loving free spirit - a free and very talkative spirit.

Tonight, however, this pillar of wholesomeness sat purposely looking out the passenger side window, mentally preoccupied with something that wasn't making her happy.

Jason considered Callie's blank stare and withdrawn demeanor. It was placing him in a difficult position - one most husbands try to avoid. She could be tired...or could be not? He considered asking if something had upset her, but dismissed the thought as lame and one not likely to bring casual comment. Then he remembered Renae had a very short skirt on and he was fairly sure Callie would have noticed, too.

Deciding to offer the topic up as a conversation starter and conjuring up a most friendly voice, he said, "What was on Ms. Clarke's mind with that itty-bitty dress she had on? Your dress is too short if you have to keep tugging at the hem all night, don't you think?"

She returned conspicuous silence interrupted by a rather loud and extended sigh. Now completely aware this ride home would not be pleasant yet still unsure of exactly what caused this attitude, Jason clung to the faintest hope that maybe it centered on someone other than him. In his most sensitive sounding voice he asked, "Callie, are you upset with me?"

"Upset! Shhh...what do you think?"

There was no longer any doubt; she was definitely angry - and angry at him. Experience had taught that she was ready to vent; the only remaining questions were -- When and how much? He thought of trying to manage a potentially seismic event by gently bringing forth the point of irritation - much like trying to manage a volcanic eruption. However, to save himself now, he had only to keep quiet. There was risk to that approach for the issue could fester in her mind and deepen her anger. From Jason's vantage point, there was no clear-cut winning strategy.

Reluctantly, after short deliberation, he opted for attempting to control the damage she was surely going to inflict.

"Callie honey, what is it? You are only this quiet when you are angry or frustrated with me. So, which is it? Either way, can we talk about it, please?"

"Jason, you know why I'm upset! We've discussed this before." Sharp eyes drenched with disdain briefly stabbed across the car before returning to look out the passenger side window - where she exhaled loudly again. A patch of fog expanded on the car window from the heat of her breath before slowly retreating to clear glass.

"Honey, will you please remind me?" asked Jason sincerely. Taking his right hand off the steering wheel, he reached out to touch her leg. However, even with her head turned, she intercepted the attempt at contact with a swift slap of the extending hand. *"Oh boy,"* thought Jason, she didn't even want him to touch her. With his hand back at the two o'clock position on the steering wheel, he made another attempt to probe for the cause of her irritation.

"C'mon Callie, I've thought about the evening over the last ten miles of silence and nothing stands out," he offered.

Turning her head and rolling her eyes upwards before answering, "How can this not 'stand out'? You let your so-called friends belittle you, and you pretend like you don't even notice?" Callie's voice was harsh and prickly. Eyebrows dipped low - shaped like check marks – as she questioned, "Am I the only one of us that notices that we're being used?"

"Callie, what in the world are you talking about?" Jason inquired, being genuinely surprised by the strength of her body language and voice.

"I'm talking about your act," she snapped tersely, springing up in the car seat. "You're a proud man and I am very proud of you, but when you get in front of these guys, you forget that pride and appeal to people whose reality ain't caught up with the 21st century yet." The corners of her mouth were tucked in and her eyes were batting rapidly, both signs of a well-fueled anger.

Jason felt a headache coming on. He had been suffering more and more headaches over the past few weeks, the kind that begin deep in the recesses of his brain and pulsate out to his cranium in waves.

She continued her rant: "You notice the faults of black people and are quick to comment when things aren't right, like Renae's dress." Callie paused, took a deep breath as if to reload, and then added, "But you are blind to other things."

Feeling defensive, Jason listened quietly. He considered allowing the comments to go on without response, reasoning that his silence would soften the effects of a tantrum he initially provoked. But now started, she would not be deterred by mere silence.

"And Bob Farrington! Ohhhhh, I can't stand that man!" Her vocal pitch building. "And you... you go out of your way to be his friend and he goes out of his way to offend you. All the while you sit there and smile... but Jason, I can tell your smile is forced and Farrington can tell, too. Still, he keeps pushing and pushing and you just take it all in stride. They're making a fool of you..."

"A fool," blurted Jason, his rising anger pushed forward by the acute pain between his ears. Callie's harsh words were the latest indication that she was becoming an unhappy wife. They were disagreeing about most everything and her general attitude was changing. She'd been angry a lot lately and it was beginning to wear on him.

For all he knew her constant nagging about this or that and the constant bitching about wanting to have a baby was the cause of these sudden migraines. And now he'd had about enough.

"I'm a fool?" repeated Jason in a voice vibrating with anger. "You've got some nerve! You sit there and tell me you get upset at the way I act, but the money I bring home doesn't upset you, does it? Who's looking foolish when you're out shopping for antique furniture and the latest fashions? It seems to me you like the rewards of success but you don't like the work!"

"I work all the time! So I don't bring home nearly as much as you do but that's not the point here - and you damn well know it!" she charged. "When Farrington comes into the room with that played out gangsta rapper strut and talking in that stupidly exaggerated African-American lingo, you laugh. He's been doing that same stupid stuff for all the years we've known him and you still sit there and laugh as if you seeing it for the first time. Plus, it ain't even funny and never was. It's really degrading, but because you laugh everyone else feels they can join in, which only motivates that fool to do more and more." Trying to lighten up just a little she followed with, "Sweetheart, it's embarrassing,"

Callie paused, carefully selecting her next few words.

"Jason, it's like you've become the worst kind racist - a black man that hates himself."

With that statement he slammed the brakes, screeching to a halt on the breakdown lane of Interstate 75. His brain pounded within his skull as Jason jerked the car into park. He then went ballistic as the painful head throbbing stoked the intense rage marking every word.

"What the fuck are you talking about? Hate myself? That is too stupid. What's happening is - I'm not liking you much lately. If you are so embarrassed by me why do you bother coming with me? You never really wanna go anyway!"

Jason said all that without taking in a breath, spewing the venomous words with hurtful intent. Now, he inhaled deeply, staring at Callie as she sat looking distant, inattentive and kind of disconnected. He was surprised at this reaction because, in the past, during the rare times he cursed at her, she became very upset. This time she seemed not to care very much at all.

After catching his breath and with no response from her, he ratcheted up the verbal assault.

"You're the embarrassment with that country accent. Fina! 'I'm fina do this and I'm fina do that.' What the fuck does that mean? It's not even a word and you throw it around like it's going out of style."

Anger animated every word as Jason's voice lost the usually reserved, controlled tone. With emotion cresting, his crushing headache pounded away like a sledgehammer. In the middle of comments meant for emotional harm, he felt something streak through his body.

It was a peculiar feeling in the pit of his stomach – queasy pangs not sourced from hunger or nausea. They weren't even particularly painful but they forced him to lower his voice and dramatically reduced his intensity.

Pointing his index finger at Callie he yelled with diminished strength as specs of spittle launched from his mouth, "You're a fucking ingrate. You love the lifestyle you're living! I've seen you flaunting your status as the wife of a successful businessman in front of your friends. Now you're saying I'm not 'black' enough."

Callie had hurt him with her stinging criticism. Until now, all of his yelling had not elicited a response suggesting she was equally hurt. In fact, she just sat there with eyes closed and appeared to not be listening. That made him even angrier. After a lengthy barrage, he searched for a phrase he knew would most upset her.

As the 'man-thing' scolding continued, Callie thought outside the situation. Always striving to be the good wife, she had chosen her battles carefully but lately there was just no winning with Jason.

They had a good life and were moving in a successful direction. Rather than recognize the collaborative effort to achieve this life he seemed to think he had done it all. This smugness was becoming intolerable as it centered on his career ambitions. That ambition was squeezing the happiness out of their marriage; getting in the way of expanding their family even though they were in the best financial position of their lives; and beyond that it was becoming the centerpiece of their social life.

Yes, this unbridled, out-of-control ambition annoyed her yet it was inescapable. Callie had come to realize the need to resist its intoxicating effect on her husband. She had begun to do so by trying to regain the position of equal partner - not be further subordinated by this monster ambition.

As Jason continued to shout a question crept onto her conscious. How much longer could she take this current existence - He, she, and this dividing ambition? Having some time ago tuned out the verbiage and eventually entering a deep, prayerful meditation, she exited that place, and heard:

"If you don't like the way I am, I can send you back to the ghettos of Chicago where I got you from. Maybe you can find a man that's black enough for you back on the West Side."

"You didn't get me from no where Jason, so you can't send me no where!" Callie snapped as a glistening reservoir welled in her eyes. "You from that same block in Chicago 'cept you think you grew up on Michigan Avenue."

Tears, pausing briefly in her lashes, spilled out over each cheek. Gathering under a now quivering chin, they plummeted down in large droplets. A circled stain widened with each descent onto the collar of her blouse.

At once satisfied and saddened by the sight of her crying, Jason checked his mirrors, looking for an opportunity to pull back onto the highway. He revved the motor of the Lincoln Town car and, after putting it in drive, took a deep breath and attempted to gain better control of his rage.

Looking at the left side view mirror, he tersely added, "You sound and act like you're still in the ghetto. I've grown past that Callie, and I ain't looking to go back to that hellhole."

Callie sat silently for a while, mad enough to tell him the cold, hard truth about his delusional priorities, but instead chose a different way, stating as calmly as she could, "I sound and act like I'm proud of where I am, where I've come from and who I am. You sound and act like you're embarrassed at being black."

The hardening positions exhibited in that exchange was the culmination of resentments pent-up for weeks and more. Verbal parry, verbal thrust - a battle of perspective without retreat. They would be the last words spoken between them that day. Jason pulled onto the highway, glancing at Callie wiping her eyes and sniffling with emotion.

That confrontation amounted to a tilt of their parallel realities toward convergence. An impending collision could be minutes, days or weeks away, but it will surely happen. At that point, there will be change. Their individual humanity will reflect the change positively or negatively; constructively or destructively; honestly or purely intellectually.

The next few miles of highway found Jason feeling remorse for the things he said, especially the: 'If you don't like the way I am, I can send you back to the ghettos of Chicago where I got you from' line.

He was sorry he went there for he loved this woman and could not imagine life without her. It was an immature, *ad hominem* response to her charges and he was already regretting saying it. Still, it was too early to apologize but too late to take back. Little did he know that he would be the one going *bon voyage*.

Chapter 3

The argument was over but the rest of the ride home was like the very beginning - thick with unspoken tension. To break the silence, Jason turned on the radio, as he reached he was reminded again that his stomach was not fine. Being so upset with Callie, he wondered if he had strained an abdominal muscle, all the while hoping it was not the early stages of an ulcer.

After arriving at home, the atmosphere was so unfriendly between them that they avoided each other the rest of the evening, eventually preparing to sleep in different parts of their attractive split-level house. It sat on a half-acre wooded lot in one of the better-maintained Stone Mountain subdivisions. The upstairs held the master bedroom complete with a large whirlpool tub. A countered, three-walled, mirrored dressing nook sat outside the door of the bath area.

Callie commandeered the bedroom during their infrequent spats. Clothes left on his side of the bed and other clutter were clear indications that he was not welcome to sleep with her. She was an impeccably neat person and Jason knew the bedroom looking unkept coincided with a bad mood. On this particular night, he had not even bothered to go upstairs. The not welcome sign was expressed all over the house in ways the blind and deaf could understand.

There were two other rooms upstairs. They had converted one into an office; it was a well-used room. Jason often brought work home and Callie printed programs and flyers for the

Sunday morning service and various other church functions. The other was rarely used. It was set up as a workout room but mostly stored overflow from the master bedroom and the office.

The middle level contained a dining room and living room. They sat directly above the two-car garage, an area usually cooler than the rest of the house. The drafty location was a comfort in the summer but required long-sleeves or a sweater even in the mild Atlanta winter. The kitchen, also on that level, was a huge rectangular room, its length as long as the dining room and living room combined.

Within the interior sat an area with a hutch-like half-wall looking out over the den on the lower level. A slate mantel, extending from one corner to the other, displayed their most cherished items - wedding pictures, vacation souvenirs, fancy figurines, and a couple of autographed baseballs. The centerpiece was an antiquated leather-bound Bible that had been passed down to Callie by her family before they moved from Chicago.

The Bible was in good shape and had a print date of October 1904. A metal bracket compressed the pages tightly in place and probably accounted for how well preserved the book remained over the years. Though fragile, it was beautifully maintained and a valued family heirloom.

A double sliding door off the kitchen led to an elevated deck. Jason and Callie built a trellis along three sides of the deck then added a thin net mesh as cover. He was proud of their work. It was a nice, warm night so he decided to sleep there this night.

Jason let out the futon in a corner of the deck, positioned a pillow, sheet and spread while muttering: *"Well, it won't be the best night's sleep, but it should be adequate."*

Not sleepy just yet, he unlatched the screened porch door, flipped on the outside light and stepped down the stairs. Stored underneath the deck were assorted parts and pieces of projects completed, in process, or abandoned altogether. Reaching the ground, he walked out into the yard, revisiting the words exchanged with Callie during the ride home that evening.

Jason's head began to pound out another headache. Of more concern was that curious feeling in his abdomen. It had become more intense; his stomach was growling as if he'd not eaten all day.

Walking into the yard, he triggered the motion sensors prompting mounted floodlights to bathe the backyard in illumination.

All of a sudden a white bird, flying very low, swooped over his head. It was squawking and flapping its wings in a frenetic pace as it circled the yard multiple times, much lower than normal. He was drawn to the unique luster of this avian creature.

Turning slowly to keep his eye on the bird's flight, Jason thought it a seagull before quickly dismissing that idea because he had never seen such a bird in his sub-division. Moreover, in his experience, if there was one seagull visible there were scores more in the general vicinity. He looked around finding no others in sight. Landing on a corner of the screened deck, after a few more seconds squawking, the bird settled-in to a calm perch.

It cast a weird light, one that competed in brightness with the floodlights anchored atop the house. Jason believed the creature to be looking directly at him. How strange that a bright white bird would be flying this way on a pitch-black, moonless night. He mumbled to himself: *'Hey, birds don't fly at night, do they?'*

Seconds, or more, passed by with Jason and the bird locked eye-to-eye. Not long afterward the dove-like creature took flight. It flew diagonally upward, directly overhead. Tilting his gaze to track the flight, Jason saw the bird disappear in the cloudless sky. Its path did not angle out of view toward the horizon; instead, it rather quickly vanished, straight upwards.

Jason thought it a bizarre ending to a bad day. Noticing his stomach had settled as he walked back to the house, he was relieved. Back inside, he dressed for bed with eagerness for a good night's sleep. After all, the next day was Monday and he wanted to get to the office early.

Laying down on the futon, Jason pulled the sheet up to his shoulders, rolled over and fell asleep.

Sunday Night

The Flight

Chapter 4

A spectacular panoramic view appeared out of nowhere.

Jason gained consciousness in the midst of being aloft. He was moving - no flying at a good clip and with a hint of purpose. The direction was unclear and the destination unknown, but there was something relaxing about these happenings. Gliding comfortably, he almost lazily thought, "What in the world is going on?"

Not only airborne, he was moving fast, zooming over milky white clouds. No more than a foot or so below him, they steadily rolled by. He did not seem to come into direct contact with them as he whizzed through the air. Never anything he enjoyed, the necessity of air travel brought on unease, especially as he realized this flight was very different indeed.

In increasingly alarming order, Jason noted there were none of the usual noises associated with air flight, no hum of jet engines or cramped spaces, no seats or overhangs, no aisles or armrests, no windows or fuselage. Finally, the ultimate realization - there was no plane.

Heightened senses advised Jason to brace for the worst. But there was something soothing about his surroundings and his predominant emotion was calm, full of wonder and wide-eyed curiosity. His was the vista of a bird in flight, unencumbered, free of all the usual obstructions.

A strong citrus aroma was in the air, but it was not tart for the smell was sweet and very, very pleasant. It was mysterious and

Jason mentally ticked off a series of items that might emit such an enticing smell. Much like a freshly cut bouquet of flowers, the smell was everywhere.

Still, the origin of the wonderful aroma remained tantalizingly out of reach, even as he was romanced by its joyful redolence. It was not until he registered sound that he was finally able to pull his thoughts away.

His attention turned to a low decibel swooshing. He saw nothing that would generate such unusual noise. It was light and fine as if a floor were being swept with meticulous timing. At exact intervals - every second, maybe every second and a half - that brushing sound occurred. It was very precise - having the constancy of a machine:

Swooooooosh.   Swooooooosh.   Swooooooosh.

The gentleness of the sound affected him like a meditative chant intending to relax. Both smell and sound were so pleasant, so consistent that, after a while, Jason was able to concentrate beyond them both and onto the incredible visual splendor materializing before him.

His wide view was, in scope, comparatively narrower in height, and the edges blurred, making them non-discernible in all directions. There seemed no way to adjust his straight-on view. From side to side, as far as he could tell, was a near perfectly straight horizon, consisting of pure white, gently rolling clouds below and beautiful blue sky above. A flawless, straight-line streak of grayness seamlessly separated the two.

He was enamored by the magnificence of the blue sky. It was not a simplistic hue, but rather, a color unlike any he had ever seen. Smitten by its majesty, the color's depth was incessant; it cast a velvet shadow – regal and royal – while being simultaneously shallow to the point of translucence. It was a vivid, memorable sight. As he thought back on the most breathtakingly beautiful scenic views he had witnessed, this was twice that.

The clouds below resembled bunched cotton balls, frayed at the ends yet soft and still. Appearing buoyant on the surface and thickening in density underneath - a wispy, dry-ice kind of haze rose off their surface. The smoke lurked just above the surface, restricted by some unseen boundary from climbing further upwards.

Amazingly, there was now no indication of the sun whatsoever. Yet he was traveling in light. The illumination emanated not from one specific area in the sky but rather radiated up from the clouds so close and perfectly white beneath him.

Jason thought he was traveling at very high altitude, although he could not confirm that sense for there was no opening in the clouds to allow a view of the ground.

He recalled a different sensation when he had traveled in the stratosphere. One such flight was to the island of Okinawa, Japan, while in the Marine Corps. He flew over with one of his Marine Corp buddies, Kevin Baylor. Jason had not seen Baylor in years, but his fascination with the visual brilliance, in conjunction with the fragrance and the gentle swooshing, hypnotically affected Jason's psyche.

It ushered in a period of reflection. He thought back to the last time he had seen Kevin:

Kevin Baylor burst through the squad bay doors, "Yo Jay, you here?" Listening to music through headphones, leafing through a textbook, Jason did not hear him. Kevin stepped around the lockers bordering Jason's private space and flicked off the stereo power. Startled, but more annoyed, Jason looked up, taking off the headphones.

"What in the hell you doing, Kev?"

"Yo man, you ain't gonna believe this, but I just got my fuckin' orders to go back stateside," Kevin yelled with glee in his voice.

"What!" Jason closed the book with a thump. "How do you get to fly back before me?

"The Air Wing rotation is different from you grunts."

"Fuck you, Mr. Hotshot!"

"Now-now, that sounds bitter. Or, is it jealousy?"

"Shut-the-fuck-up Kevin. When you flyin' out?"

"Saturday, but I won't get to Minneapolis until Monday."

"Damn! Monday? What are you flying in, a balloon?"

"It's that International Date Line. You know it works in re-verse going back the other way. We got to Japan the same day we left California, which was weird enough, but now it's like it's going to take two days to get back home."

"Yeah, but it'll be the same long, miserable 22-hour flight time. Coming over, I thought we'd never get off that plane."

"Except on the way back we're gonna stop in Hawaii instead of cold-ass Alaska. Maybe we'll have a layover and I can get me some hula dancer strange."

"Ah Kev, you are stuck on that one-way street. Too bad you're going the wrong way."

"You need to get on this street sometimes."

"I get on it plenty enough."

"Speaking of which, we're going out Friday night for one more Okinawa drunk fest. And, I need a favor."

"You know I can't go, I have class on Friday Nights."

"Man, fuck them books for one night, come and celebrate with yo' boy."

"Can't do that, Kev."

"Okay, but you can still do me this favor."

"You're a short-timer on this Rock. What more could you want?"

"I need a loan – not much though. I should be able to get drunk and laid for 50 dollars."

"Fifty dollars! You must be out of your mind. I'm not giving you that much money. You're leaving before the next payday."

"I know but I'll pay you back when you get back. I'm going to Minneapolis and you're headed for Chicago. They're close, we'll find each other while on leave."

"No fucking way!"

"Jay, you've loaned me money before – or should I say loan-sharked me money. I always paid you."

"Yeah, but we're both on this tiny island in the middle of the sea. Where the hell could you go?"

"Come on man, I got one more in me and I'm tryin' to get it out. Be a friend, Jay. We'll see each other stateside. We could end up in the same duty station."

"Or, we could be nowhere near each other."

"No matter, I have your Momma's phone number and you have mine. You'll be back by the next weekend, two weeks at the latest."

"Yeah, that's probably true."

"Exactly, now loan me this 50 bucks. I gotta go back to work."

"Kevin, I need my money back, plus an extra 25."

"Seventy-five dollars! I thought it was 65 for 50.

"It is. But, I'm trusting you over a longer distance."

"What, you'll be back to America by time we get paid again."

"Longer space not longer time."

"All right Jay, but you're being a real asshole about this. Why don't you come along with us? Your books ain't gonna get cold if you don't hold them one Friday night."

"Can't do it, Kev," Jason reached for the lockbox in his locker. "I've got final exams; it's the last night of class. Are you gonna see Meriko before you leave?"

"Fuck no! She's talking crazy shit about going back to the States with me and getting married. I had to drop that bitch in the 'gutter' and go get a 'nutter.'"

"That's real nice," Jason said sarcastically. He handed Kevin the money while asking, "This one-way street you're on, does it have any stop signs?

"Yeah, they're all turned backwards for guys like you going in the boring-ass direction. Anyway Jay, thanks a bunch. I'll call you in a couple of weeks, back in the real world. Gotta go now though."

"All right Kev, see you back home."

He never saw or heard from Kevin Baylor again.

Pulling his mind back to the present, Jason compared those two transpacific flights to what was happening now. The high altitudes of both were unique experiences. With cerulean skies being a function of sunlight on the earth's atmosphere, Jason again searched the upper expanse of his vision for some indication of the sun. There was none, but he was becoming annoyed for he could not adjust his head.

There is a limit to how high one can see, for to really see upwards, angling one's vision is not sufficient. To truly look up, the head must move.

Those minor frustrations were put aside as visional consistency re-enforced original calmness, allowing Jason to spend time reveling in the tranquility associated with gazing upon the azure.

Chapter 5

The serenity disappeared as Jason' senses were shaken. There was a sudden, strong sensation that his path began to descend. Instantly focusing down to the clouds, they suggested this perceived shift might not have happened at all.

The clouds' position caused him doubt for they remained six to twelve inches below. However, there was something very different about them now; the general appearance of the clouds had changed dramatically from their calm, benign early state. They were now moving around leftward in a clockwise motion. The force and strength of their movement was stunning.

A low hissing accompanied the gentle swoosh. In addition, that sweet citrus fragrance, so beguiling earlier, was noticeably lessened, gradually intruded upon by damp, musty notes.

On his guard, Jason saw a darkened point in the clouds just in front of the horizon. To better examine this strange happening, he focused his sight, peering out at what looked like a rounded-edge hole, angling down, like the eye of a hurricane. The clouds emptied down what looked like a drain being sucked into a vast canyon of darkness.

Jason realized this new development just as he resolved the uncertainty of a slant in his flight. Those clouds, lurking just below, were now distinctly angled downward. Further out they were churning as if being stirred with a gigantic spoon by some unseen power, their texture gradually changing from cottony white to menacing-looking patches of pewter gray.

That wondrous, wide-eyed curiosity which accompanied this voyage from the beginning gave way to previously anticipated concern as a wave of adrenaline inundated his thinking. He considered that maybe he had died and was about to descend into a hellish abyss. This disconcerting possibility triggered him to try and physically resist the forward motion.

He instructed his body to stop, yet there was not the slightest hitch. This complete failure caused him to become more determined with his instruction, commanding his body to alter this course. The mental effort had no effect. He just could not move. Continuing towards the drain and, with less space between, it was the obvious target.

Nowhere near cloud-like anymore, he passed over darkening matter. Having transformed into organic-looking material, there were greasy patches looking like animal fat checkered throughout. Light flashed brightly underneath the mass portion. An electric crackling sound accompanied the flashes, which had the chaotic suddenness of lightning, but there was no thunder.

Moving closer, Jason saw the vortex spinning violently downward. A few yards away, unmatched panic encroached.

"But how could this be?" He wondered to himself, *"If I'm dead how can my mind be so lucid, post-mortem?"* That thought forced a realization to become prominent, as if released by some elastic restraint. He had not felt or seen evidence of his body. He had not sensed touch or feeling of any kind. Nor had he seen his nose, shoulders, arms or legs. Having clear sight, there was no visual evidence of his glasses.

It was as if his consciousness alone was on this trip.

Jason was swept into the circular vortex fearful for his mortal soul. He was as scared right now as he had ever been. Could he be in some *Charonian* vessel, Hades bound? In the crevice, his flight path changed sharply - dramatically angling downwards. And there was now a thunderous noise as if the route to wherever was facing strong resistance.

That noise, similar to a waterfall - constant and full - enveloped him from every side, but there was no feeling of turbulence. His perception that the trip had turned rocky was based purely on his visual sense - every area passed seemed unsteady and jumpy.

"Dear God, where am I going?" Jason tried to speak the words but did not feel the effort was successful. He did hear an echoing voice that sounded very much like his. It distracted his concentration - how strange to hear one's own voice reverberating as if being spoken from some other place. Despite the hollow echo and distant source amplification, he was sure it was his voice - slightly dissembled, but his nonetheless.

Rushing deeper into the narrowing confines, he traveled through a noisy tunnel lined with ugly gray matter. If this were a plane, it would be traveling nose down at increasing speed. Free of any containing compartment, Jason seemed to be accelerating downward, head first.

Down he went.

Steadily down! Flashing images along the walls of the vortex were spinning and flipping as if part of a television set that had lost its horizontal hold. Flickering by at rapid speed, only a few were recognizable. There he was getting his first hit in Little League; his mother as a young woman, she looked to be pregnant; then his grandfather who died back in 1965. Jason had only remembered him by the pictures he had seen at various family functions over the years.

Relentlessly down! Was this his life flashing before him? If so, why were so many images unrecognizable? None were of any part of his recent life. Where was Callie? How could the single most important person in his life not be part of the final act? Jason tried to remember when he last told her he loved her. Not being able to so now spawned great sadness and a deep yearning for another chance. He fought against an it's-too-late despondency settling in.

Unceasingly down! Overwhelmed, he wanted to close his eyes. Though he had sight, far as he could tell, he hadn't even blinked. Moving through thick, moist, dense tubing - the area around him was getting tighter and tighter, a cause of great discomfort.

There seemed not enough room for his body to get through. When some part of the tube got especially close, he searched for the ability to feel it, but to no avail. All the while his sense of smell was imbued with contradicting aromas - a damp, human musk, interchanged with a unique, newborn baby freshness.

Distorted vision and that loud, roaring noise drove him to the brink, then - silence. He exited the tunnel and was back out in the open.

The visual change brought a sense of freedom, due largely to a shift in the flight's direction. He was now under the clouds, gliding once again, and more importantly, not in some fire and brimstone hell but descending back to earth.

The sun, now bright and large, was readily apparent in the sky even as the land area below was unfamiliar and certainly not Atlanta. This place was rural and heavily forested, completely devoid of buildings or other structures.

His travel speed accelerated sharply and soon the relief of not emptying into some netherworld was gone. The closer Jason got to the ground, the faster he seemed to travel and now there was a real danger of smashing into this unrecognizable countryside. With the trajectory of a meteor approaching Earth, he raced across the sky toward a group of people walking a dirt path.

They were black people, barely dressed. There were men in front walking in a V-shaped flank position. Jason saw women and children in protected positions walking within the V. One of the women looked like his Aunt Cherry. Always one of his favorites, she'd died a few years back. She looked to be a younger woman here. As he went past her, Jason realized he was headed directly for the man in front.

Without a hint of deceleration, he was about to crash into the back of the man's head.

The Kwame Nkrumah Memorial by Ferris Shelton 1998

By Ferris Shelton 2017

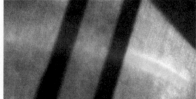

A High Ground View of El Mina

By Ferris Shelton 2016

Monday

The Behavior

Chapter 6

Jason snapped awake.

Resembling a sit-up, his upper body sprang forward off the futon. The blanket that covered him last night was strewn across the porch. He must have lost it early in the night, which might explain his body being chilled to the bone. Beads of sweat fell down the back of his neck, further matting his pajama top to his skin.

As a child he had dreamt often, but since becoming an adult his memorable dreams occurred much less frequently. Even so, last night's dream was vivid.

Jason recalled the depth of color and the realistic physical dimension of his sleep. This bizarre experience nearly scared him half to death. Just before he had awoken those strange people that were in his way looked as if they had no idea he was close - even as he bore down on them. Whew, Jason thought, what a wild dream.

After a few minutes, having calmed down, he decided now was not the time to ponder too long on the trivial. His rationalization was that it was simply looking backwards at something with zero relevance to what was important now. Switching to work mode, he began getting ready for his day. He liked being the first one in on Monday mornings.

Without thinking, Jason started up the staircase to begin his morning routine before remembering the confrontation with Callie last night. Stopping, he opted to get ready downstairs and waited to hear her showering before quietly retrieving all the things needed upstairs so as not to have to go back.

Moving briskly allowed him to be dressed and out the door without a word being spoken between them. Though he wanted to share the dream's details with her, he thought it best today to return the silent treatment he assumed would be coming his way.

Jason was confident they would make-up sooner rather than later because their marriage was solid. Although there were some hurtful things said last night, it would pass because he and Callie were indeed soul mates. True, things were not going well between them of late, but their marriage was happy and he was not 100 percent sure how they had gotten so far from that happiness.

This recent friction with Callie dampened his mood while driving in to work. Dourly, Jason drove the slow lane, mechanically braking in delayed synchronicity with the tail light of the vehicle in front of him. He was in emotional purgatory between contentment and frustration, betwixt a comfortable lifestyle and something bad creeping up on the other side. Sure, they had married young - she 21 and he 22 - but to him that just proved they were meant for each other.

Both were born in Chicago. It was a small miracle that he and Callie had not known of each other much earlier in their lives. Jason was sure they had never met, for how could he have missed this person that so captivated him? Yet, as they discovered over the years, they attended the same school for a while.

And they lived within a couple of city blocks of each other at three separate times. For a lengthy period of time, as children, they even attended the same church. Yet Jason was certain he'd never met or even seen Callie during those years.

'Oh no,' thought Jason, blue lights in the rearview mirror. He reflexively went on alert, causing the car to tug abruptly to one side. Where did this Georgia State Trooper come from?

Distraction with Callie caused this inattentiveness. As he pulled over, Jason prepared his presentation while putting his hands on the steering wheel. The officer exited his vehicle and walked towards the passenger side door.

Viewing the officer's approach through the side mirror, he watched the officer unsnap his holster and lift the belt up on his hips. Jason thought, *"Oh boy"*.

"May I see your license and registration, sir?" offered the trooper as the car window wound down to its base. Jason collected those items, mentally chastising himself for that moment of anxiety because he was not a criminal and had nothing about which to worry.

"Here you are, officer," Jason said, handing him the items.

"Do you know why I stopped you this morning?"

"No sir, I don't. I may have been going 70, but traffic was faster. I'm in the slower lane."

"No, you weren't speeding. Your left tail light is out." The state trooper went back to the cruiser.

Sure this would be no more than an inconvenience, he returned to his worries. After being honorably discharged from the Marines, Jason had gone home to Chicago. He was more than a bit nervous about returning to civilian life and planned on pursuing his college degree, which he'd energetically started while in the service.

Jason believed they met originally about a year after he returned to the Windy City and, although he had never admitted to anyone, as far as he was concerned, it was truly love at first sight. Callie was fine and unique.

Her physical appeal was real right away and, as he would later discover, their psychological connection was true and complementary. Mischievously fun when in the mood and thought-provokingly serious when called for, she was perfect for him. Strong and rooted, Jason found her a loving person with an enchanting internal glow.

Callie' touch was as inviting as a warm bath on a cold winter's night. With an attitude that could be misconstrued as stand-offish, underneath an urban-hardened shell was a pearl of the Nile, his *Nefertiti*, and he had sensed it early on.

"Here's your license and registration. I'm just giving you a warning so you'll have seven days to get it repaired. And one other thing, Mr. Scott, buckle up – it's the law."

"Thank you, Officer. I'll have it fixed within that time."

As the patrolman went back to his squad car, Jason put on his seat belt and pulled back onto the highway, smiling with confidence. That's how you bring on good fortune, he thought. If you present yourself as if you are trouble then you are likely to find it. Thus, he had designed his presentation with politeness, intelligence, and articulation.

It was this strategy, he thought, that highlighted the advantage he had over Callie. He knew what it took to succeed in the America in which they live. He knew the game and played by the rules. And, on top of that, he was winning.

He and Callie's early courtship had been filled with anxiety. His car broke down on their very first date and they had to take a cab home. Eventually the clumsy awkwardness smoothed out and after a time they became an item.

He remembered the day he realized she was really special. It was August 7th, eight years ago, at 3:30 PM. Together they sat in Wrigley Field from 12:30 until 3:30, as it slowly populated to capacity, waiting for a game.

The starting time had changed at the last minute (he had been so embarrassed because he was the baseball fan) and they only had themselves for entertainment for three hours. Callie and Jason talked and laughed the whole time. There was comfort developing in their more private interactions and he was surprised how at ease he was with her - and how natural she seemed to be with him in public. By the time the game started Jason almost wanted to take her somewhere quiet so they could continue talking. He knew for sure – that day – that Callie was the girl for him.

He proposed a few months later and their wedding was a few months after that. All in all, after being in fairly close proximity to, yet somehow avoiding, each other for 20 years, they met and married within a year.

Chapter 7

Jason pulled into the office complex of Edwards Industries, went through his morning arrival routine, and settled into his office when the phone rang.

"Good morning, Edwards Industries, may I help you?"

"Hi Jason, are we still on for our 8:30?"

"Hi Bob. Do we have an agenda? If not, I have an A/P batch that's going to be late if it's not done soon."

"Yeah, that's part of what I want to talk to you about and some other things. Instead of the whole half-hour, I think we can review the few things I have in fifteen or twenty minutes."

"Fine, but you're on the clock."

"Not yet. I can't get there until 9 o'clock."

"Alright 9 it is. See you then."

"Right."

"*Great!*" Jason thought to himself. No sleep, fighting with Callie and now Bob Farrington. It was time to make the adjustment and to focus on work, but his love's unhappiness did not leave his mind immediately. Her disgruntled attitude was unwarranted as far as he was concerned because nothing had really changed in their relationship. And that's the way he liked it. But she wanted all kinds of change, most of which, in his mind, would be too much.

Five years ago he was offered a relocation package to move to Atlanta. Though all their extended family was in Chicago, they decided to leave. It was an exciting time, for although he had traveled extensively while in the Marines, Callie had never left home. After convincing her that this change would be good for them, Jason was determined to make it work.

That change was in pursuit of a larger goal. Their progress could be measured by the fact they were settled into their second home in the Atlanta area. Two years ago, the move from Decatur to Stone Mountain roughly doubled their home equity. In March Jason had been promoted to office manager. This left him one rung away from the business success that he felt was his destiny.

Callie made a smooth transition to metro Atlanta, working at a community center as an activity administrator for pre-high school students and was a major player in the Urban Angels program designed to assist in building the self-esteem of young women from mostly dysfunctional families.

She was very involved with the church, participating in several auxiliaries and sang in the choir. She kept an impeccable house and was a great cook. More importantly, she was his best friend - that being the bedrock foundation of their relationship.

He loved Callie with all his heart. Even so, there were certain times when he thought she was becoming a professional hindrance. As he climbed the corporate ladder, her once cute idiosyncrasies were, in some business situations, becoming a liability. And it seemed that over the past few months their closeness had begun to erode.

Yes, they had married young, but that was not a factor in the developing chasm. The basic problem was philosophical. He wanted to go for the brass ring and he was willing to sacrifice for the business success he craved. She, on the other hand, was probably a little homesick and determined to start a family.

Jason felt having a baby now would stifle his career. Articles abound detailing the costs of raising a child in America and he thought it better to land at a specific financial plateau before taking on the responsibility of a child. He often made the point that he preferred to wait a couple more years.

It was a point that had no leverage with Callie these days and he was becoming frustrated. Jason rationalized that most career-minded people waited until their mid-thirties to have children, but she refused to even try to understand his reasoning.

He saw Bob Farrington approaching his office. It was nearly 9 o'clock and he had not begun preparing for their meeting. Spinning to his computer, Jason clicked to the A/P processing module, quickly running through the keystrokes needed to generate an open payables report in hope that the techno-voiced "yes" would sound soon after Farrington arrived.

Farrington walked along the side wall of the general office area, and the numerous cubicles and workstations contained therein, without saying a word to anyone. Jason found this behavior odd though common with Farrington and others. How can you walk past people you work with for the first time of the day and not at least say 'good morning?' He had witnessed that sort of thing countless times but considered it one of life's unsolved mysteries. His feeling was that it cost nothing to be polite.

After not saying a word to anyone in the general office area, Farrington burst into Jason's office with such overtly friendly exuberance it bordered on hubris.

"Hi ya Jason. What a great party at Clay's house last night, eh? The shiitake appetizers were fabulous and the prime rib and shrimp scampi were awesome."

"It was a good party. Thankfully, it ended early enough so that I'm fresh this morning. I'm facing a few deadlines this week," replied Jason.

"I know you've got to get A/P out and process a payroll this week but, I've got a few things to go over with you, and I'd like to talk a bit about last night."

"Last night?"

"Yeah, I had a conversation with Clay, before you and your wife arrived, that I thought you might be interested in."

"Oh," Jason put aside the stack of invoices. "I guess I am interested"

"Well, first let's take care of today's business. I talked to Renae this morning when she came in. She's wearing another tight outfit that is far too revealing. I've cautioned her about the inappropriateness of some of her office attire. Now, I'm beginning to lose my patience."

"Bob, she's a young woman who likes to dress the way young people dress. What's the problem with that?"

"The problem is this is an office, not some hip-hop hootchie club. And you know the difference between a white woman and a black woman, don't you?

"I think I've heard that one..."

"One's on the cover of Playboy and the other's on the cover of National Geographic. Sometimes we have important people walking through the area and she is just not attractive enough to wear the things she wears with that big butt pushed into clothes too tight. It's just too much. And man-to-man, those lips of hers ain't good but for one thing and it ain't procreation, brother."

Farrington let loose a hearty laugh as his soft, jellyroll stomach jiggled. The laughing caused his body to whip up and down as if he were riding a galloping horse. Jason thought the words mean and unnecessary. He allowed Farrington to get a good head start because he knew the part he would play.

Obligingly, Jason smiled, and then exhaled a forced chuckle before finally letting out a real-sounding laugh. He had mastered these contrived acts of amusement. It was an expedient approach to interacting with some; the indignities suffered were balanced against the perception of getting along with everyone. Still, there were times when Farrington could test that strongly held conviction. This was turning out to be one of those times.

"Anyway, I'm sorry, that may have been a bit crude. But, ahhhh, I set up a meeting with you and Renae for today at 3:00 regarding this matter. You need to talk to her and tell her this will be considered a verbal warning."

"A verbal warning? On what grounds, Bob?"

"She can't be prancing around here looking like a streetwalker."

"Have you passed that by Human Resources?"

"No, of course not. We'll need to document it as poor work performance."

"Well, she doesn't work for me; I know nothing of her work performance. She works in your area, why don't you talk to her?"

"Yeah, I know, but I don't relate well with her. She has all these black mannerisms and jargon that I can't hope to understand. And I don't want to either," Farrington stated.

"So, you want me to do your dirty work."

"Exactly. But here's the reward. At the party last night Clay informed me that he is considering taking a position back in Ohio."

"Really. And how does that reward me other than the obvious."

"The obvious?"

"Never mind, it's a joke."

"Oh yeah, very funny. Anyway, if he leaves, he's going to recommend me for the vice president position and that's where you come in. I'm going to move you to my old position and get you away from some of this grind – A/P and payroll - and put you in a more important position with better exposure to the company gatekeepers. It will be good for your career."

Jason felt his insides burning free like a windswept wildfire. How dare Bob be so confident that any vacated position will naturally fall to him? And he could not believe that Clay would recommend Farrington in such a way that circumvented the process of search committees and internal mobility.

Where was the open process that Edwards so passionately espoused? Did others know that Clay was considering moving on; was he the only one in the dark or was Bob privy to information that was being closely held? Either way, Jason realized he was not going to be given a shot at the position and that was plain.

Bob continued. "You're a good man and we need more like you. I plan on bringing you right up the ladder with me as my right hand man. You're black but a different kind of black. Clay and I were talking the other day and we both agreed that you are more a BASP. Instead of a WASP or a white Anglo-Saxon protestant, you're more a black Anglo-Saxon protestant. Get it – BASP. So you're in good here and if Clay leaves, I wanted to let you know that I am going to move you up with me."

"What makes you so sure you will get the vice president position?"

"Who else? Terri is ready to retire in a few years and Joe... well...Joe does not have the make-up for a vice president job. He is damn good at what he does but he doesn't have that certain *gravitas*."

"And you do?"

"Of course I do. I've been groomed for the position and feel I'm ready. Don't you?"

Jason thought, "*The arrogant bastard didn't even include me in the assessment of the potential people next in line.*" What he said was, "I don't know. I guess you're as ready as any of us."

"More my man - a lot more. Anyway, take care of the Renae issue without rocking the boat. You know, explain things to her in that language you guys speak. What's it called again ebony-nomics."

"The term is *Ebonics* and I don't necessarily speak..."

"Whatever. Just take care of it," Farrington stood to leave before adding, "And don't forget to process my expense report. I'm going golfing Wednesday. Care to join us?"

"No, I have work to do."

"I knew you wouldn't, but we're a foursome already, Clay and a couple of guys from sales. Listen we have the A/P supervisor candidate meeting tomorrow. I think we'll be able to get you from under all this paper shuffling work and maybe leave more time for golf."

"Yeah, right," retorted Jason, mono-toned just enough to conceal rising resentment.

"All right that's all I have. See ya later."

After Bob left the office, Jason sat fuming, focused like a laser on the back wall. Seconds later, however, he smiled and saw what he considered the brightest of bright sides. With Farrington being so confident concerning his imminent promotion, all he had to do was accept the fact that he would move up again soon and be that much closer to his goal. Sure, he'd like to be considered for the vice president's position but he was recently promoted and thought it better to bide his time patiently.

Bob had confidence in him and that is exactly the position he needed to be in now. By combining steady, consistent performance with patience, his prospects were bright and the roadmap was clear. Soon he would become vice-president and Callie would be proud.

That was a tough ride home Sunday night. Her comments had made him very upset. She was more at ease in all black social settings than he ever was. He had struggled to fit into his own community from elementary school and high school on through his adult years, so it was natural for him to go with his strength. That aspect was understood and she had accepted it for years. It was part of their attraction as a couple.

Chapter 8

Throughout this day he performed the more mundane, thoughtless tasks of his job, while his mind centered on the problems of his marriage. He was beginning to feel, for lack of a better term, that they were from opposite sides of the track. Although he and Callie were both black and lived in the same community all their lives, Jason thought the metaphor worked, although in a nontraditional way. One reason they had not met as children is that she attended the district school from elementary to high school while he had, most of the time, attended an integrated school.

In fact, he had been a pupil on the bus of the Chicago Board of Education's federally mandated school integration program. As children, she attended the district school, Spencer Elementary, and he was bused to Josephine Locke Elementary on Chicago's far North Side.

To Jason's way of thinking their different academic background was the crux of the problem they were having lately. Callie did not have enough experience dealing in European-American social and business circles whereas his experience began early in his life.

Until fourth grade, his first year at Locke, they were on the same side of the social and academic track. One of his earliest childhood recollections was being in third grade at Spencer where he was part of a group of boys that hung around, horsed around, and got around most of their learning responsibilities.

As he thought back to those days, he had definitely been a follower. At the tender age of seven or eight peer influence pulled on him with the strength of a locomotive engine. A shy, quiet, big kid for his age, he was all but drafted into this group of young rascals. Aiming to please, he would do almost anything to receive acknowledgment. Toward the end of that school year the boys stumbled onto something that could have had very bad consequences.

One day, just as the weather began heating up in Chicago after a typical windy and snowy winter, the boys did not return to school after their one-hour lunch break. Jason followed the group of juveniles away from the school grounds but was absolutely petrified that his mother would eventually find out about his truancy.

Together they roamed the neighborhood and dispersed around the time school let out. At home that evening, Jason was on edge waiting for the phone to ring and spill the beans about his escapades earlier in the day, but there was no call.

He and his delinquent friends talked the following day and discovered no one was called and for all intents and purposes they had gotten away with skipping out. Being rambunctious boys and not much into school, this was a fantastic discovery. However, it was also fraught with danger. Playing in the streets as a child when everyone else was in school was not the safest thing to be doing.

He remembered a time when he barely escaped being hit by a car. And another time, after spending all afternoon throwing rocks through the windows of a large tenement building, he narrowly evaded the clutches of a very irate tenant. They stole candy at a number of local stores and got into a lot of mischief. No one at Spencer ever called their parents.

The group disappeared after lunch once or twice a week for the final six weeks of the school year. Not even the teacher seemed to notice, or if she did, she didn't care.

During this time, Jason and his renegade friends were tracking down the criminal path running directly through the halls of Spencer Elementary. But the following year began the busing program and his school experience changed profoundly. He remembered begging his mother not to make him go all the way up north to attend that white boy school, but his mother knew where the quality education was being dispensed in Chicago at the time and it was not at Spencer.

Ring.

Startled, Jason looked up at the clock, it was close to three o'clock. Being a single ring he knew it was from inside.

Ring.

"Hello."

"Hi ya, Mr. Scott. You ready to meet or do you need mo' time?"

It was Renae Clarke.

"No, no, I'm ready. Is it a convenient time for you?"

"Yes it is. I'll be right there."

Renae entered his office five minutes later as Jason quickly decided to approach this conversation in a friendly way, eschewing the hard company line. Because he had spent the past few hours worried about Callie and their problems, he had no script ready and had not prepared an outline of topics to be discussed. This was a situation for which he had no heart. It was unnecessarily bureaucratic. If Bob wanted her gone, why didn't he just fire her? Why throw her in his lap? He took a deep breath and attempted to dress his voice with young person vernacular.

"Hey, how ya doin' Renae?"

Renae's eyebrows arched as she responded, "Uh, fine Mr. Scott."

"Have a seat." Jason raised his arm and directed her to the seat at the side of his desk.

"Thanks. Mr. Farrington said you wanted to speak with me?"

Walking by his desk, Jason noticed Renae's clothing and yes the stretch material of the skirt was tight and short but certainly not out-of-bounds with what was being worn by women her age. She was in her mid-twenties and, as they used to say, she was a brick house, with small, full breasts on top and shapely hips and backside below.

She presented herself well - hardworking, smart and full of life. Renae enjoyed her R&B and hip-hop music sometimes a bit too loud in the reception area but never when visitors were around, at least as far as he could tell, but he didn't know her well at all. She was younger, single, and far too type-A for him to have even attempted more than a casual, friendly rapport.

As she sat down and looked up at him, Jason noticed that her lips were nearly identical to Callie's in size and fullness. Were he at a different station in life he could be smitten; with her being young, attractive, single, and child-less - Renae would certainly be worthy of a second look. However, he was neither young nor single and hadn't bothered to look once.

One would have to sift past the dolled-up presentation - including the latest fragrance not quite masking all her natural essence, to get to the real person. By all indications, she was a good girl, somebody's daughter and sister that attended church and talked about it at work while trying to live in a world that pulls in opposite directions. Jason sat up in his chair and mentally pushed the on-button as that last heartfelt point was kicked aside, along with all the rest, because they were beside the point.

"Yes, Mr. Scott," Renae sat down and crossed her legs.

"Relax; this is not a big deal. I just wanted to find out how you are doing and if you like it here at Edwards."

"Well I'm doing fine and yes, I like the job. I prefer to be busy and the phone never stops."

"Don't I know it."

An awkward silence followed, Jason remembered how he hated not being prepared for meetings, even with subordinates.

Seconds passed with both looking off from each other in obvious discomfort.

"Sooooooo, is there anything else you wanted to speak with me about Mr. Scott?"

"Come on, Renae lighten-up. I just want to chat for a while. Find out how things are going and if you have anything you want to talk about. I just wanted to catch-up. By the way, why don't you call me Jason?"

"Okay...Jason."

"So what's on your mind? How is your life at Edwards?"

"Nothing really, Mr. Scott, I mean Jason, everything's fine with me."

"You don't have any questions?"

"You know what, I do have a question. What is that thing in your shirt pocket? No matter what shirt you wear there is always something in the pocket and I was wondering what it was?"

"It's my calendar – a mini palm pilot. I use it to make sure I'm at the right place at the right time."

"Oh, one of those. My brother has one but I think his has a phone, too."

Another nail-scraping-the-chalkboard period of silence during which time Renae fidgeted in her chair. She looked at the door suddenly and then abruptly sat-up at full attention. Renae had brought in a pen and notepad and after a few more seconds she put the pen to pad and looked up at Jason.

"Do I make you nervous, Renae?"

"No not really, but Mr. Farrington tells me you want to meet with me and I don't know what to think. I do wonder why you didn't tell me yo' self. And now all of a sudden you want me to call you Jason and you tryin' to act all friendly. I been here a year and half and you always been Mr. Scott. But today you 'Jason' and I'm wonderin' if I'm in trouble."

"I wouldn't exactly call it trouble."

"Well, what would you call it, exactly?"

"Communication."

"About what?"

"Well Renae, you are on the front line and you're the first person people see when they visit Edwards. There has been some concern expressed about your choice in business attire."

"My attire! You mean my clothes? What's wrong with my clothes?"

"There's nothing wrong with them it's just that we would like to see you make an adjustment."

"An adjustment! What kind of adjustment!?"

"Perhaps wear longer skirts that are not as tight as the one you have on today."

"Oh, so that's what this is about. Mr. Farrington been making comments about my appearance for a while. I don't think he likes me. What am I suppose to do Jason, buy new clothes? This is what I like to wear and I am covered-up every day."

"No, it's not that you are exposing too much. It's not that at all. It's just that you're a healthy woman and the clothing choices you make seem inappropriate for this environment. You are nice young lady but maybe you should just dress a little more conservatively."

"But Jason, since I was hired here from the temp agency, I'm the same size and wear the same style clothes. So, I don't git it. What's the problem?"

"The problem is that some people think your clothes are too tight around the hips."

"Oh, I see. Jason no matter what I wear my hips are going to show. I'm a good-sized black woman. This is Mr. Farrington ain't it?"

"That's not important."

"It's important to me. What am I suppose to do, hide myself in oversized clothes? That ain't gonna work. Does Mr. Farrington object to these white girls in here coming to work with low-cut tops and sometimes even bra-less? I've seen more nipples here than at my sister's and she's breast feeding twins. I ain't never been in here like that – it ain't that serious."

"It's not about that. Why can't you just make an adjustment?"

"Does the way I dress affect my work? – No! I dress this way because I'm not just here at Edwards. I commute and maybe I want to attract a nice looking man. I can't do that wearing no burlap sack."

"Renae, this is a business."

"And I do my job, Mr. Scott. I saw your wife at that boring party last night. How did she get you - by wearing a white shirt and a pocket protector?"

"Again Renae, that's not the point."

"The point is that these white girls can go around exposing their tits but a black woman has to hide her ass. This ain't right, Mr. Scott. Are you going to all the women or just me?"

"No one else dresses as provocatively as you, Renae."

"That's not true. I know you seen some of these low cut tops in here."

"Yeah, but they haven't been brought to my attention."

"Then we back to Mr. Farrington. He doesn't like me Mr. Scott and there is no wardrobe adjustment that's gonna change that."

"I don't believe that's true"

"You don't know as much about that as I do, Mr. Scott."

"And I don't want to know, Renae. I'm asking you to adjust and go along with the program. You don't want to be viewed as an employee with an attitude problem, do you?"

"No I don't Mr. Scott. I need this job, but you sound like you asking me to not show my blackness. Look at me and tell me how am I gonna do that."

"It's not about blackness; it's about playing to expectations. Would you wear these sorts of outfits to church?"

"What I wear to church is not yo' business. But like you said 'Edwards is a business.' I don't have a business relationship with my religion. I have a personal relationship with God."

"Okay, I definitely don't want to get into all that. Will you please try to make this minor adjustment?"

"I like this job Mr. Scott but I don't see why I have to try the impossible."

"And what is that?"

"To be less black."

Jason thought being unprepared was putting him on the defensive.

"Is that all Mr. Scott?" asked Renae with a bitter tinge coloring her voice.

"Yes, Renae," Jason responded, feeling very uncomfortable with the entire conversation. "You're doing a good job. Just make this little shift and you'll be fine."

She uncrossed her legs, stood and left the office without saying another word, clearly annoyed. Jason clasped his hands and shook his head. He was telling her right - it's too bad she was too young to understand. Her background was not clear but he thought she may have been local - which in Metro Atlanta, Georgia is a rarity - and was actually born and raised here. Bright-eyed, excitable, and with real upside potential, she lacked guidance.

Minus this newer generation's in-your-face self-confidence, he thought, she might be better prepared to accept his advice.

Chapter 9

Looking back over his life, he considered himself fortunate to not have turned out different. Too many did not survive the Spencer-like experience. Thinking of the final few days of third grade at Spencer, he recalled one in particular, when he actually stayed on the school grounds after lunch and took a spill during recess. He learned an important life lesson after his knee went the wrong way and stayed there.

There were two souvenirs from that fall on a gravel-covered courtyard that are still visible. Slightly more noticeable was a horizontal welt of clumped scar tissue on his knee to this day. The other, a crescent-shaped area of an incision to fix muscles and tendons with names he never could pronounce – that wound, though healing smoothly, never regained the original skin tone.

That incident happened over twenty years ago but he held on to the memory. Over the years, the injury grew to symbolize what happened whenever he has had to operate in all-black environments. It served as a constant, physical reminder that if possible, avoid all black settings.

Never has a scar healed so physically yet festered so psychologically.

The following September his mother enrolled him at Josephine Locke Elementary school. It was an eye-popping experience, for this school was clean and all the windows were intact, unlike many that were boarded-up at Spencer. Students played all-across or touch football in spacious manicured grassy areas. Falls and tumbling shenanigans were part of the fun. However, on the very first day there was a harrowing experience for the kids traveling by bus to Locke. At the time, Jason did not understand all the hoopla.

The bus-launching site had so many people - some were parents, but most were curious on-lookers and media. Still, all that was mild compared to what awaited the bus on Chicago's North Side. After arriving at Locke, a few people standing in front of the school began booing. When the students and bus attendants disembarked some of the people pelted them with eggs. There was no real attempt made to injure any of the children and the people throwing the eggs were soon moved away.

As the news of that morning's events spread throughout Chicago, Jason's mother was livid. She left work early that day to meet the bus at the meeting site on the return trip. Angry but unbowed, she had Jason back on the bus the next day. The novelty of integrating Chicago's public schools was eventually accepted and the school year settled into a normal routine. After the early commotion subsided, he found, in academic challenges, a lifelong motivation.

Locke was not only proverbially across the tracks but also in an entirely different world. From the outset, he experienced challenges at the strange new school that he had not encountered at Spencer.

Jason discovered he could compete scholastically at Locke and this propelled his self-esteem skyward. When he studied and put out maximum effort, he got very good grades. Some of the students bused to Chicago's North Side did not do as well and he began to feel it was his responsibility to become the standard bearer for those under-performers. Jason was determined to prove to the teachers at Locke that he was a black kid who could compete at a high academic level.

The evolution from follower to leader had begun.

Comparatively, thriving at Josephine Locke Elementary School became easier than surviving the off-school social hours back in the neighborhood. Young Jason was having a more difficult time communicating and connecting with his contemporaries – especially the males. While working hard at his diction, to improve his grades, and to better assimilate at Locke school, that same effort was isolating him in inner city Chicago.

Because he was beginning to stick out in an awkward way in black social circles, Jason had to fight many times as a kid growing up. His years at Locke had placed him on the other side of the Great Divide, that yawning canyon between the children being educated at Locke and the children being processed at Spencer.

As a preteen Jason had two close friends named Michael Fisher and Allen Cosby. They were little league baseball teammates living in the same neighborhood. As children, they always wanted to spend the night at each other's houses, clocking in as many hours together as their parents would allow. Whether shooting marbles, playing basketball, or hanging around the block, they were constant companions.

The three were bused to Locke for five straight years. They were true road warriors. Though he could not recall exactly how long it took each day, he knew they spent a lot of time on the bus. This may have been where their friendship jelled. By the time they were in seventh and eighth grades, the three were inseparable.

However, after graduating from Josephine Locke Elementary School, he gradually drifted away from his two childhood friends. Jason went on to a high school on the far North Side while Allen and Michael decided to go back to the neighborhood for high school. By the time he graduated most of his social time was spent away from the West Side.

For the past few years, he fancied himself a diplomat for black people. As he encountered whites he would put forth his best, most impressive persona. He felt that other blacks would do well to follow his lead. Even with this philosophical outlook, there had been times when he felt like a fish out of water. It was as if he were in the right movie but with the wrong part.

More than once, usually after particularly uncomfortable social encounters, Jason would secretly wish he were white.

The work day seemed endless and Jason spent much of it seeking some rational reason why he and Callie were falling out. When it finally came to an end, he felt he had met a minimum requirement of productivity. Edwards was temporarily under-staffed due to the resignation of his accounts payable supervisor a few weeks earlier. Jason thought it a prime time to show his higher-ups he could handle all aspects of his responsibilities, even during tough times. After bringing accounts payable up-to-date on the mainframe, he went home to an empty and dark house.

Callie had choir practice and would be late coming home from church. He didn't even make an attempt at dinner; he was far more tired than hungry. Turning on the stereo in the bedroom, he switched the station from gospel to jazz. During stressful times jazz had a way of easing his tension. Preparing for bed, he smiled while thinking of sleeping in his own bed without look-ing as if he was giving in to Callie. As an added benefit, if she were there in bed when he awoke the next morning, they would be on their way to making up.

It would be nice for them to be friends again; he was tired of fighting, tired of arguing and just plain tired. After stretching out on his bed, sleep quickly overtook him.

Monday Night

The Capture

Chapter 10

Vibrant, drum-driven music burst through silence.

Percussion rhythms entertained, but with strange accompaniment. Voices from near and far expressed merriment and celebration, not with words but other utterances. Exuberance was evident though it was too dark to see. Between every bass drum beat was a bongo, and between the bass beat and the bongo were various other notes that seemed to find just enough space in-between. Cowbells were rung, wood blocks tapped, and a kettledrum or xylophone-sounding instrument being played up and down scale.

Jason found himself feeling happy. In the past, whenever such a feeling of contentedness took over, his mind and body would tingle. There was a definite sensation happening now – a deep internal appreciation for this musical score – yet there were no physical manifestations of this ecstasy.

The joyful noise reminded him of times in his life when his spirit would swell inside during a particularly moving gospel song. Listening, he wondered how music lacking lyrics, or any known arrangement, could have such deep effect.

The symphonic richness was intoxicating and the musical composition unique. Every sequence of beats seemed different, as if the music was attempting to communicate in a language of its own.

The peculiar cadence occupied the night. For night it was as Jason found himself outside with a full moon in view. It was large, hanging low in the sky, yet there was not as much visibility as there should have been with a large, nearly yellow moon. Extreme darkness gave way slowly and he noticed silhouettes of objects moving out in the distance. That strange movement, though confounding, seemed far away.

Soon enough his eyes focused on that movement, helped by faint light situated in the background, while his mind reveled in the melody.

The driving bass drum and sweet treble percussions chimed out crisp and clear; it was high fidelity music. The natural reverberations were too near to be reproduced sound. This was a live concert with people playing instruments in the immediate vicinity. It was up-tempo; made more cheerful by the other, happy, human sounds.

Jason thought the music diverse. There was a reggae influence, the way it emphasized in-between beats; there were classical elements in its well-ordered melodies; there were jazz rifts with seamless shifts in tempo that keep enthusiasts hanging on the precipice...and that ever-constant, funky bass drum.

It seemed to correspond with the beat of his heart. That exact correlation soothed Jason to the point of complete relaxation. He was enraptured by the rhythmic pulses.

A spirit-induced peacefulness allowed his mind to wander. Seeking some comparison for the harmonious beats, he thought of a young drummer at their Atlanta church home named Tyrone Polk. He was a teenager and a musical prodigy. There were other drummers but no one played like Tyrone Polk - his style was distinctive. Jason thought back to the church service on Sunday before the argument with Callie. He had slipped downstairs heading towards the church kitchen and arrived at the door just as Callie stepped out.

"What are you doing down here?" She asked sternly.

"Oh hi Callie, I'm hungry," Jason said defensively, knowing he should not have left the service. "I thought maybe there would be something I could get quickly in the kitchen."

"You shoulda ate something at home!"

"I would have, but you were rushing me."

"Cause you so slow, if I didn't rush you, you'd still be there."

"Yeah, but then I wouldn't be here talking to my beautiful wife, would I?"

"What? Jason, don't get on my nerves."

"All right honey, I'll get something to eat later." Jason leaned down and kissed her cheek. "Where is Tony this morning?"

"Nobody knows," said a forgiving Callie, reaching out to re-center Jason's tie on his shirt. "But Tyrone is here so we gonna be jammin'."

"Oh, that's for sure. That boy is really unbelievable."

"You know Mother Polk tells me he has never had a drum lesson. He tapped on empty cartons and other things all the time as a child. And he was soundin' good."

"I know he gets my foot tapping all the time."

"She bought him a child's drum set one Christmas when he was seven and the boy was playing like a pro by early summer. He could hear a song on the radio and play it the next time it came on." The church organist began to play an intro upstairs.

"Yeah, it sounds like the natural is warming up."

"Oh my God, I gotta get up to the choir stand. Bye, sweetie."

"Don't hang around too long after service, now Callie; we have to get to Clay's house for dinner."

"Oh yeah, I tried to forget."

"Come on honey, it'll be fun and we won't stay too long."

"Mmmm Mmmm..., okay see you later."

Back upstairs, Jason enjoyed the choir's spirited singing and Tyrone's gifted drumming. He was a tall, lanky kid with an emotionless face that would serve him well at the poker table. He was well-mannered and always polite, conveying the impression of being only mildly interested in the goings on around him. That apparent smugness evaporated when seated in the drummer's chair - where his face acted out the effort of every stroke.

However, ten Tyrone's couldn't duplicate the polyrhythmic drumming heard all-around him. The music was beautiful; more peaceful than delightful; more divine than both.

Boom,
Tinkle-bang, tinkle-tankle, bang
Tinkle, bang, tinkle-tankle
Boom,
Tinkle-bang, tinkle-tankle, bang
Tinkle, bang, tinkle-tankle
Boom

Like two dancers stepping together; angling and kicking in concert with each stride, his heartbeat stayed with the bass. It wasn't reacting to the music - it was the beat. Synchronized, they transformed to a quickened tempo in unison, just as he detected dramatic movement ahead. Not really sure how, Jason saw a discernible thinning of the space between him and the light source some distance away.

That light was better visible now as it sat low, no more than six or eight feet off the ground. It appeared to be getting brighter...or closer...or both.

There was an inconsistency in the way its rays reached his eyes. Never entirely unobstructed, the light traveled through a maze of activity. Now, with fewer blockages, the area's activity commanded his attention.

As his eyes better focused, he began to comprehend the things happening within view. There were fewer objects between him and the light. Realizing people had moved away from their positions in front, Jason's eyes strained for opportunities to see past the last few people moving about.

His heart palpitated after skipping a beat and then accelerated. In the back of his mind he was fully aware of the bass drum
keeping perfect time.

Relegating the music to the background of his consciousness, Jason concentrated on piecing together what was happening in front of him. Silhouetted images were oftentimes block-
ing his clear view. People very close to him were the primary
obstructions.

Their head-bobbing and arm-waving caused the light to flick-
er. Suddenly the group of people bobbing and weaving directly
in front of him danced out and away from his position – leaving him completely dumbfounded. Their departure was abrupt.
As if on cue, they rushed off in high-stepping, hand-waving delirium. Now he stood in the open; able to see, for the first time,
exactly what was going on 40 feet away.

And what he saw defied belief.

There were scores of people dancing in a clearing as three
fiery torches burned in the center. The blazes, sitting within
golden perches lodged in the ground, were about six feet apart,
flaming toward the stars for there was not much of a breeze.

The people dancing in the circle were a study in motion, all in
coordinated rhythm with the music. They followed the instruments with their movement - never moving opposite the beat –
in perfect syncopation. Feet kicked on the bass notes and arms
waved with the percussions. A full-body gyration linked the two.

Jason stared at the dancers, taking note of their appearance.
No one was completely dressed. Some wore cloth, but most of
the men wore furry animal pelts around the waist. Some of the
women wore loose material that swayed from side to side with
their dance movements - while a few were topless. None of them
seemed the slightest bit self-conscious.

Nearly everyone wore beads and most wore gold. Thick nuggets were strung together, allowing them to move freely as the
dancers moved. There was a beautiful assortment of ornaments

worn around the neck, the waist, the arms, and legs. As people danced, the jewelry clacked together providing a low-decibel but clearly audible sound, adding a unique tone to the mesmerizing percussions.

Chapter 11

The scene was startling. Time to make sense of it all was short, for soon after the people in front departed, Jason perceived movement again. This time, however, it was not other people moving, it was him. Though he felt no physical exertion, his arms were waving and his legs were kicking out in front of him.

A deep voice called out from afar and suddenly his body rocketed forward in hyper-motion. He could see his knees rising alternately and his hands and arms swinging about, although he did not feel the physical effort needed to make such movements.

Jason saw himself skip out towards the center as a cloud of dust surrounded him. The smell of dirt and smoke was joined by something new. It was both musty and human. The bewildering scent stymied his mind but his body kept on moving.

Without warning, there was a ruckus to the right side. The musical tempo changed unexpectedly, becoming eerily erratic, as all the instruments came to a staggered ending, except that bass drum.

Then something happened - he spoke. His brain had not sent a command to his mouth to speak; still he spoke. He had not formed his lips for words nor prepared his throat to utter sound because he could feel neither, yet he spoke.

His ears heard it in a way that only occurs when hearing one's own voice. His nostrils smelled the breath as the words came forth from his mouth. What Jason heard himself shout, in his own excited voice was, "Obrony bi woh!" The term was totally foreign to him.

While running away from the mayhem, Jason shouted those strange words louder, many times. The phrase seemed to alert the people still dancing but not paying close attention. A festive dance, once organized and orderly, quickly turned otherwise, with people frantically bumping into each other and yelling.

In the middle of all the excitement, two loud bangs caught Jason off guard.

They were not from the solitary drum for they were muffled and hollow like that of a mortar. The people close by stopped, turning abruptly. His forward motion came to a halt and his head looked toward the sky.

A net propelled out and aloft now affected the view of that full yellow moon. It seemed to float over the area where the people had minutes earlier been dancing in an atmosphere of revelry and merriment. An instant terror wrenched his consciousness as unhealthy fear descended along with the net.

Everything in his view jumped violently. In slow motion he saw he'd run into another man and they tumbled. The impact of the collision caused him no pain, yet when he landed on the ground, sights and sounds suggested he hit very hard. A voice – shockingly, his voice – cried out in pain.

The net ensnared Jason within its thick, merciless rope and cross ties. The sheer horror of being trapped in a net was pervading every brain cell. Being free of pain, he tried to make his body struggle against the purse-seine capture, but a body that had been unresponsive to any mental stimulation continued to ignore his thoughts and wants.

This body, lying on the ground, apparently injured by the fall, could only further cramp itself by crawling limp-legged under that all-constraining net.

Voices approached from the right. They were animated calls from men fanning out, shouting in yet was still an unrecognizable language. When they got close, Jason saw a man preparing to strike him with a stick.

Thwap!

A loud thud sounded upon impact, followed by an agonizing exclamation. Feeling perfectly still, Jason's body acted out incredible physicality, writhing on the ground.

'What the hell's going on...?' Jason's mind, only momentarily distracted by that query, noticed through the netting, another strike coming his way. This one toward his forehead.

African Band Stand set-up LaBadi Beach, Accra Ghana by Ferris Shelton 1998

The El Mina Courtyard by Ferris Shelton 1998

Side View of El Mina by Ferris Shelton 1998

Cape Coast Slave Castle by Ferris Shelton 1998

Tuesday

The Capitulation

Chapter 12

Callie awoke with Jason cowering by her side.

"Jason! Jason what's wrong with you? Why you sleepin' so rough?" He heard her, but as he opened his eyes, he had not fully come to his senses. For the second straight night a numbingly real dream occupied his sleep. The first had been kind of distantly amusing - a plane-less flight, beautiful scenery, and that eerie whirlpool of a hole in the clouds. But with people and actions appearing to happen in real time, last night's dream was outrageous; much more disturbing.

Sweat-drenched pajamas clung to a body not close to rested while nervous energy percolated in his veins as if he just went through a wild, exhilarating real-life experience. This weird feeling caused him to hesitate. His mind was in LaLa Land, not quite able to let go of the nightmare, though he was free from its grip. Concentrating on the comforting familiarity of his surroundings, Jason tried to convince himself that the dream was not, in some strange way, an alternate reality.

"Sweetie, are you O.K.?" Callie pressed, seeking a verbal response. She thought his eyes looked dazed and confused.

"Yeah Callie, I'm fine," said Jason groggily, finally focusing on Callie in the dim morning light. "I just had the worst dream."

"I know Jason. About five o'clock this morning you just about kicked me out of bed. What's goin' on?"

"Nothing honey, I've just been under some stress at work since Chubby left. Lately, Edwards has been a real a grind."

Jason turned to her adding sincerely, "And plus, sweetie, I don't like arguing with you. Callie, I'm so sorry."

"Oh sweetie, I know and I'm sorry, too" Callie replied, "I said some really mean things."

Jason began feeling better. He had known they would make up.

"Yeah Callie, but I deserved it. I didn't take your criticism well, and when I get defensive, I can get pretty stupid."

"Ain't that the truth," Callie smiled in sarcastic agreement.

That adoring smile told him all was forgiven. Thinking of consummating the make-up, he reached for her and surprisingly she allowed him to pull her close. He did not think she would for he was rank from sweating during the night and he had terrible halitosis in the morning.

But when he gently sought her lips, she was willing. They kissed warmly and affectionately. Sensing he might move her even further, Jason reached for her pajama bottoms, getting them down to her thighs before being rebuffed.

"Oh no, you're stinking wet with sweat. You need to go brush and wash everything," stated Callie turning her head, playfully pushing him away.

She stood from the bed as he moved his hands down her hips. There was a prominent birthmark on her left buttock and he patted it as she pulled away. Cutting her eyes back, Callie sashayed out of his grip with an exaggerated wiggle in her walk, pulling up her pajamas. The birthmark was a half-dollar coin size mole that lifted slightly around its circumference and settled toward the center. It resembled a crater.

Early in their relationship, she had been self-conscious about it. To Jason, it was but a small blemish on an otherwise perfect posterior.

Falling back against the bed, he was thankful to be in her good graces even as the damp sheets put the dream front and center again. Before prepping his mind for work, he decided to cut back on spicy foods and caffeine, hoping that would alleviate the sleep problem. Jason tried to ignore the sudden, spectacular aspect of his recent nights. They would not be ignored for long.

Commuting to his office building in Atlanta's Buckhead section was an unenjoyable necessity as traffic around Atlanta was very congested. Too many commuters drove excessively fast, causing many accidents. He felt as if he'd survived a demolition derby with the safe arrival at work each morning.

Ordinarily the walk to his office was spent planning his day, but this was no ordinary day.

He could not recall ever before having dreams that felt so real. The people last night seemed authentic, the dancing and that suspended net were incredibly real – even now the experience was extremely clear in his mind. Though it was a cool morning, his body began to overheat.

Jason entered the office building thinking *"enough is enough,"* switching his mental focus to work. Stepping into the elevator, he distracted himself by thinking this was decision day for the accounts payable supervisor position. Chubby Ragans, the previous supervisor, had left the company a couple weeks earlier. As with many other issues at Edwards Industries, they proscribed to the "Reactive School of Management" theory instead of the "Proactive.'" A month's notice had been given, yet Chubby was still allowed to leave without a replacement trained or even hired.

Being a high-energy type with a keen eye for details, Chubby was a real asset to the accounting area. Of course, that was not her real name - he could not remember if it was Deborah or Dionne. Everyone referred to her by that nickname, which itself was a misnomer for she was a tall, slender African-American woman. The irony was such that she refused to be called anything else.

Born a corpulent cherub, her nickname was assigned early on by older siblings. Though despising the moniker as a young girl, she grew to love it when she slimmed down later in her life.

Along with his other duties, Jason closely oversaw accounts payable after she left the company. It had been a tough stretch and very time consuming, but that extra effort would be winding down because there were two finalists for Chubby's vacant A/P supervisor position.

An exhaustive interview process whittled a large, talented field down to two well-qualified candidates. Jason's choice was a middle-aged African American woman with three years of supervisory experience named Wanda Rodgers, who was willing to start immediately.

The other candidate, a young, very attractive European-American woman named Diane Scosia, was attempting to step up in responsibility. Her work experience consisted of five years in a large centralized office. Sharp and ambitious, she had probably outgrown her only post-college position. But a major strike against her, as far as Jason was concerned, was that she required a two-week lead-time. Both finalists were qualified enough that either would do fine.

Timing was a major consideration in the hiring and Jason believed he'd get the person he wanted. Wanda Rodgers had that additional edge of being more experienced. He considered her a better risk for long-term employment. Ms. Rodgers, unlike Diane Scosia, was less likely to use the position as a stepping-stone to bigger and better opportunities.

The elevator doors opened just as Jason considered the matter all but settled. A/P help was on the way as early as next Monday. Confidently turning the corner from the lobby to his wing of the building and using his security card to gain entrance, he stepped through mahogany double doors into his comfort zone. Terri McGowan, the comptroller, sat at the reception desk, fingering through an appointment book and scrolling a digital calendar.

"Have we started cross-training?" Jason asked jokingly. Looking around the reception lobby, he was strangely relieved at not seeing Renae.

"Good morning Jason. I've lost a meeting time and Renae has bailed me out before. I hope she made a better note in the master calendar than I did in my personal one.

"Terri, if you miss that meeting there will be plenty of others."

"Don't I know it," chuckled Terri. "Around here it seems we can never have too many."

"Yeah, but some are more productive than others, like today when we select the next A/P supervisor. I won't be sad to turn managing the vouching process over to someone else. The luster of batching invoices is long gone."

"I checked the monthly balances this morning and you look to be doing fine. Maybe we don't need to hire anyone, just leave it in your more than capable hands."

"Not funny, Terri. Not funny at all," Jason shuffled backwards shaking his head in playful disagreement, adding with a smile, "You have a great day. See ya at 9:30."

"Yeah thanks. What time does Renae get in?"

"Around 8:30, I think."

"Well, that gives me about 20 minutes to find my meeting time and get out of her space."

Chapter 13

Jason walked through the inner office area saying "good morning" to everyone, a routine started many years earlier. He believed the greeting helped foster friendly working relationships. Cultivating this idea of a positive business image, he maintained a sense of professionalism throughout the workday. He hated when the business was not being properly attended to.

And he really hated wasting time. To emphasize this point he would sometimes place his watch down on his desk when meeting with his staff.

Ten minutes before the operations meeting, he and others began congregating in the large meeting room, dubbed conference room 'won.' The name was word play as the only other meeting room was titled 'too.' The meeting attendees were Clay Calhoun, vice president of operations; Terri McGowan, controller; Bob Farrington, general ledger manager; Joe Gaudio cost/financial analyst; and Jason, office manager.

Clay Calhoun was the 'Boss', a burly and boisterous man from eastern Ohio. He job-hopped to climb the corporate ladder, yet when he shared his story, he told of pulling himself up by his own bootstraps, portraying his life and career as that of a rugged success story. Jason considered him a talent-thin, silver-tongued bullshit artist who would blow blue smoke through 40 feet of coiled garden hose if he thought it would make him look good.

He was the kind of person that treated people meanly, especially restaurant wait staff and others he considered doing menial jobs. He would often proclaim not to be a 'computer person' or 'reader' or 'math person' when it was convenient to camouflage his lack of substance. He was one hell of a golfer though, and could spend hours talking about his low handicap.

Next in the hierarchy was Terri McGowan, a world-class nice person. Terri was a native Georgian, from somewhere south of Atlanta - a town called Jackson. Being brilliant and mild mannered, Terri worked at Edwards Industries for nearly a quarter century and was Jason's mentor, having strongly advocated for his most recent promotion. Being tough yet fair, demanding and understanding, she was a good corporate steward, leading with a real human touch.

She'd made a fabulous career for herself and was nearing early retirement age, of which she planned to take advantage. Her grandchildren promised a more physically active lifestyle than the challenging 10-hour days she spent at Edwards. A gentle person by nature, Terri's approach to most business matters served as an oasis of pragmatism in what could be a cutthroat, short-sighted corporate culture. She was highly respected for being fair and benevolent, even as she navigated through a pool of sharks.

Joe Gaudio was an introvert with small hands and an even smaller personality. Were anal retentiveness a musical instrument, Gaudio would be a virtuoso. If you walked into his office, threw a wad of paper and missed his trash bin, Joe could get flustered to the point of obsession, for his space was museum-quality neat. He only used No. 2, old-fashioned pencils, saying he had become comfortable with their feel over the years.

Certain items had to be the right brand or he could be very unhappy and has stormed out the building to an office supply store to get exactly what he needed. Every paper or folder on his desk was perfectly stacked. He once spent too many minutes completely distracted, in a meeting room full of people, wiping away a cup ring on the conference table.

Jason, Bob Farrington, and Joe Gaudio were all at the same level in the company's organizational chart. Farrington was the senior man, having been with Edwards Industries for 10 years.

Bob Farrington was a man who considered himself very principled. His politics, which he wore on his sleeve, were staunchly conservative, to the point of being religious. There were pictures of both Ronald Reagan and William F. Buckley Jr. on the wall of his office, along with multiple copies of the National Review and American Spectator on his table. Being from a small town in Mississippi, without roots in Georgia, he networked with an uncle in sales to land the Edwards job, relocating immediately after college.

Farrington and Jason were about the same age and apparent friends, or so it appeared to most people who knew them both. In fact, Jason resented Farrington's arrogance and was somewhat offended by his aloof, self-righteous attitude. Still, he was good at business and that demanded Jason's respect. That respect translated to wide tolerance for his shenanigans and, at times, accepting abrasive ways and actions.

Farrington's personal attributes were of little concern for they had to work together, and Jason was determined to maintain a productive, professional relationship.

In Jason' mind that did not mean being subservient but rather meant not sweating the small shit. However, with a person like Farrington sometimes the small shit grows from a molehill to a mountain.

Callie disliked Farrington like poison, mentioning many times she thought him a blatant racist. Jason dismissed that opinion as trivial and insignificant. And even if he were, Jason would prove himself a capable, competent colleague, therefore upsetting any and all preconceived notions about people of color.

It was his self-assigned diplomatic mission since his days at Locke School – to prove that he was a black man that could compete and succeed. In addition to that, Jason realized an interpersonal sparring match with Farrington would not further his career, so he played along with, and yes, some might say, played up to his conservative co-worker to keep his eye on the bigger prize - that next promotion level.

The meeting's usual jovial camaraderie over coffee and doughnuts progressed to serious business when each person updated Clay Calhoun on their particular areas of responsibility. Half-hour in, the topic of filling the accounts payable position was opened for discussion.

"Well, we've narrowed the field to two candidates for the A/P super," asserted Calhoun after stating a decision would be made today. "Any thoughts?"

The process required everyone to give his or her impression of the finalists. Jason sat leafing through papers, holding back, not wanting to look pushy. Eventually there would be a voice vote and he hoped the decision would be unanimous in favor of Wanda Rodgers.

After Calhoun posed the question, there was a short period of silence until Joe Gaudio offered, in unsure, soft tone, "I think both are excellent candidates, but I liked Ms. Rodgers. Her answers to questions were more exact and thoughtful." His voice faded as if he felt his comments were not being well received.

"Well they were both good interviewees, Joe," said Farrington in an overly loud voice, "but Ms. Scosia seemed more of a go-getter, and being better educated she might be more receptive to training. I thought Wanda Rodgers was a bit disorganized, appearing jittery when responding to detailed questions."

After those comments, Jason looked up from the papers to measure the reaction of the others to what was said. He was not surprised at Farrington's vote for Diane Scosia. On other occasions, he had intimated to Jason that he thought the office was getting 'too black.'

Now it was his turn to give his opinion of the accounts payable candidates. For Jason, the office racial make-up was a cursory thought that was irrelevant to this decision. He had sold himself completely on the meritocracy of the system in general. To him, ability meant more than anything and that was the way he functioned.

"Well, it seems clear to me that the best candidate is Ms. Rodgers," stated Jason, "She has more experience with our accounts payable computer system and she seems more settled, possibly a longer-term employee."

"Yeah Jason, but can we really afford to hire someone disorganized?" Farrington inquired, quickly looking across the table at Clay Calhoun. "And, there is the language issue."

Reaching into his folder, Jason pulled out Wanda Rodgers' resume, "There is no indication here that she is disorganized. And I thought she spoke English well, though with a slight accent. She was born in Jamaica."

"It is precisely that accent," countered Farrington, "that would make the training difficult and constantly in need of being refreshed."

"Whoa," Jason exclaimed, sitting forward in his chair. "We are attaching attributes to her that are not indicated on her resume."

"Hold on you two," Terri McGowan chimed in, putting a hand up. "Let's not get into a spitting contest. I believe both to be qualified applicants, but we need a decision today. Jason, since this position will be reporting directly to you, I say it's your call."

With rank and hierarchical position woven through his voice, Clay Calhoun added: "But keep in mind, we need a strong employee that will not require excessive training and be able to communicate orally across all functional areas and, of course, with our vendors."

'Sure,' Jason thought to himself, the decision was his but the tide was rushing towards Diane Scosia. Saying anything other than that would not reflect him in the best possible light. He had worked hard to build a reputation as a team player. The perception of being willing to cooperate was an important component of his career goals. It was also a true part of his make-up, one kept readily on display when interacting with his business associates.

In the past, this type of decision would have been a no-brainer. His potential personal gain would have far outweighed all other considerations, especially if those considerations were for people he barely knew or were regarding issues about which he did not particularly care. If management wanted Diane Scosia, he would be an eager supporter of that position...but this time there was turmoil inside.

Ever so faintly, Jason heard the sound of drumming in his mind, forcing him to sharpen his focus. Back to the issue at hand, he calculated the situation.

Clay Calhoun was possibly close to moving on, which would position him one step closer to a vice president position which he wanted more than anything in the world. Though he honestly believed Wanda to be the best choice for Edwards, he could not and would not sacrifice his career aspirations to make this stand. Besides, he rationalized, accepting Diane Scosia might even propel him up the corporate ladder a little faster.

With that in mind, his decision was made, even as his physical discomfort increased.

Jason took a deep breath, selecting the right words for the moment. "Perhaps we do need some fresh blood in here," he stated, "someone with a young and new perspective. I don't have a problem with Diane Scosia."

The drumbeat between his ears intensified, strikingly off-beat from his heart, leaving Jason to contend with this growing distraction. For the rest of the day, he could hardly see straight. He struggled through with noticeably less energy and enthusiasm.

At home, Jason had a light supper of soup and salad, no salt or pepper. He talked very little while keeping Callie's concerns about the morning at bay by deflecting her questions towards work problems. Eventually, a lackluster Jason announced he'd be going to bed early.

While undressing, he considered those crazy dreams but quickly cast the thoughts aside because he wanted nothing to get in the way of a good night's sleep.

Switching on the dim night light in the dressing area, he grabbed a cup of water and four extra strength aspirins. Past his reflection in the mirror awaited his bed and the rest it promised. He considered the upcoming night's sleep while glancing at the alarm clock sitting on Callie's night stand.

It was still early, not yet nine o'clock. Going to bed now gave him hope that he would feel better tomorrow.

He took the aspirins, laid down and was asleep almost immediately.

Tuesday Night

The Arrival

Chapter 14

A curved sliver of light appeared in the dark distance.

That arc slowly brought on a purple-colored twilight revealing very strange surroundings. Jason was part of a procession walking in triple file. With barely enough light to illume his next step, he tried to hesitate, but his pace was quick, uncoordinated, and most importantly, outside of his control.

He walked on a sandy beach, with a group of men not only in front but to his left side and rear. Something was dripping off his brow, affecting his vision. Seconds later, without mental stimulation, his hands went up to his face. Two hands were used to wipe at the fluid, because to his surprise, they were tied together with thick rope. Seeing it was blood, he waited for accompanying pain.

But there was none. Was it someone else's blood? Forcing his focus to his left showed his hands were bound, not only to each other but also to the man on that side.

A large knot between his wrist served to constrain his hands while not allowing them to come into contact. The man to the left had a similar arrangement of rope and knots connecting his two hands. The distance between the knot of his left hand and the knot of the other man's right hand was about three feet.

Tuning his peripheral focus downward, Jason saw his feet tied together as well. There were 18 inches of rope between each ankle that served to restrict his every step and connected to the man on his left, with five or six feet of rope between them. All the men he saw - those to his left and those in front of him, were tethered hand and foot this way.

Having their feet tied to the others presented a major problem, for the rope between each walker's feet was getting caught in the sand, further impeding their steps. Forced to navigate the sand and keep a quick pace, the men had to kick up first before stepping forward. The rope between their feet caused granules to spray about as it was dragged over the sand.

The light from the brightening skies seemed filtered by a fancy photographic vanity lens. A soft, hazy sheen accompanied everything in view. There was a large body of water to his right side. The water's surface reflected an orange hue from the array of colors decorating the horizon. Gentle waves rolled in next to the unfelt sand beneath his feet.

Occasionally, a stronger wave lapped in. The water must have been warm because there was no sense of wetness or coolness even as he heard his feet plopping through the tide.

The strong beach aroma battled a repugnant stench riding the frontal wind.

That semicircle of light was the sun rising. A darkened silhouette of a rather large building stood centered in the sun's low position along the horizon. Increasing brightness showed the dingy color of the building, which had most likely been much brighter at one time. Salt and sea breeze had taken its toll, leaving on it a patina of lifeless gray. The edifice was slightly askew, not exactly perpendicular with the sea.

Its look was distinctive. There were small rectangular cutouts all along the top portion that housed a line of cylinders protruding around the corner on the ocean side. They looked like old-fashioned canons. His curiosity heightened as the group of men moved closer.

On the side of the complex, at the base of a border wall, was a rectangular-shaped indent sealed by vertical wooden planks. It sat up high, inaccessible from the beach. It was the only blemish on the smooth, impenetrable-looking wall surrounding the building.

The entire complex had the look of a fortified, well-protected fortress that stood in stark contrast to the surrounding country-side - a densely forested patch of land with no other buildings or structures in sight.

Large seabirds began to excite. Most were gulls, but Jason saw a vulture - then two more, circling near the corner of the building closest to the ocean. There must have been an animal or large fish carcass nearby. That would explain the scavenger birds and the putrid odor that had become more pronounced as the tethered procession moved closer to the walls of the fortress.

Fifty yards away the sand they had been walking on changed to large, slightly-rounded boulders smoothed over by tides and time. Soon after the troupe angled away from the shore and toward the structure. Jason saw men on horseback, flailing whips, directing the movement of the forced march. Entering the building's shadow, the tethered marchers were halted, ma-neuvered in such a way as to be standing in front of the area's highpoint – a huge, dark, solid rock.

All the men roped together were black and dressed peculiarly when dressed at all. The man immediately in front of Jason had a large bump on the back of his head and wore only an animal pelt around his waist. The man to his left was naked, dried blood caked on the side of his face from an apparent wound. All of a sudden, one of the cylinders facing the ocean shot off. *"They are canons,"* Jason thought to himself as the loudest noise he'd ever heard crashed down upon him.

Jason squinted toward the sound and followed the smoke ring expelled from the recently fired cannon. A scream from somewhere in the rear, out of sight, spliced the boom's echo.

A drawbridge lowered, across the moat, and a wood-and-rope portcullis lifted behind it, allowing men to exit on foot and horseback. Jason thought he heard the distant reverberations of chinking metal.

Someone in the rear screamed again.

Jason tried to compartmentalize the commotion – to put each unseen noise into an isolated context so that he might better interpret them. Though out of sight, the sounds emanating from behind were very close and resonated with danger.

He listened: Whip! A whistling, hissing sound of something slender forced through the air at rapid speed, like a baseball bat or stick. Thwap! The impact of something being struck was akin to a boxer hitting a heavy bag while training - followed by another scream. Happening in quick succession, the next set sent Jason's psyche right to the edge.

Whip! Thwap! Scream!

The men rushing out the compound responded to the activity in the rear. Jason desperately wanted to see what was going on but he was unable to make his head turn. Finally, a voice shouted an incomprehensible phrase. Though he did not understand the words, they ruled his body's attention. With a sudden jerk, his head swung around and what he saw made his brain convulse.

A man in the middle of the fifth and final rank was being whipped by one of the horsemen. The sound he heard was the whistling of the whip on recoil, the dull, sharp slap as it tore through the man's flesh, and then that blood-curdling scream. Adding to the shock was the precarious physical position of the man. Being in the middle meant he was tied to other men - one on either side.

In their zeal to avoid the sting of the whip the two men had instinctively gone in opposite directions, leaving the man in the middle little free space to react to the beating. His weight had slumped but the ropes on his hands and feet prevented his complete fall. It was at this point that Jason turned his head. Compassion for the man being beaten eventually convinced the two connected men to move closer to each other but stay safely away from the lash.

That show of sympathy had little impact on the dire position of the man in the middle. Despite their intentions, the beaten man's position did not perceivably change. His torso pulled forward across straightened legs with arms extended forward, leaving his bare back an easy target for the whip.

The beating took on an even more savage nature. Jason was not able to bear the brutality and tried to look away but his head and eyes were fixated on the grisly proceedings. Trying to avoid the violence, despite that being his focal point, gave him a chance to notice the other men around him. Extremely sun-darkened, they all had a look of confusion on their faces. They stood grimly quiet, staring as if entranced by the flogging taking place.

A second man, on horseback, arrived on the scene with a rusty, dirty looking sword and the man employing the whip paused. The swordsman angled the animal over to the other men tethered to the victim and, after dismounting, cut away their bindings. The rope was severed at a place that left their hands and feet still individually bound. The newly un-tethered men were moved back to one side. This left the man being flogged in full view, isolated but for the man with the whip and the other, having climbed back atop the horse, holding the sword.

The whipping resumed as the rest of the group was maneuvered to maximize their viewing.

Similar to when passing a gruesome automobile accident, there was a morbid attraction to the thrashing - it was uncomfortable to see but impossible not to watch. The bloodied man, now free to squirm and roll around on the rock, occasionally yelled the same three syllables between screams. With each one, as if on cue, Jason's body trembled - somehow he understood the man's tormented language. In absolute horror, he watched as the man was beaten unmercifully.

Blood and flesh, sprayed by the whip, streaked the dark rock with red and tan-colored stripes. The screams, which had been agony-filled minutes earlier, were now reduced to whimpers. After two more strikes - they stopped altogether. He was barely alive when the horseman with the sword leapt from his steed, grabbing the beaten man's wrist bindings.

With two hands, he pulled the bloodied victim back to his horse and remounted - then dragged the battered man to the ocean side wall. He stepped down from his mount and impaled the half-dead man. He snatched the freshly wetted, rusted sword from the man's midsection before throwing him in the ditch near the corner of the building.

Chapter 15

The swordsman's actions appeared measured and methodical, as if determined to present this kill to the men in the procession. Jason had not thoroughly digested what he'd seen when his head looked away. The activity at the corner of the building was over, yet he strained to keep the area in his sight. The effort was much too difficult, so he eventually relented and focused his concentration in the direction his head was facing.

That focal point was a man – a black man – speaking from a raised portion of the beach rock. Jason had no idea what was being said yet his body and head were devoted to the words being spoken. Eventually, the man went to each tethered individual and made a statement. There, with a sharp stare piercing the interrogated, he waited for a response, either verbally or with a slow affirmative nod of the head, before moving onto the next.

When he stepped in front of Jason there was deep-rooted fear on his face. His pupils were surrounded by orange where white should have been. There were deep lines etched into his cheeks while his countenance was both serious and urgent. He made the statement in the strange, unrecognizable language and Jason realized he did not immediately respond the way the other men had, either in voice or body motion. Without control of his body, panic ascended.

Jason was willing to acquiesce to the demands of this strange man - whatever those demands were. He was afraid if his body did not give that indication he could meet with a horrible death like the one he'd just witnessed. Standing directly before him, the man grabbed his shoulders and repeated the puzzling statement, yelling it in his face. Again, he did not respond.

A sense of peril forced him to consider: *"This could be the last few moments of my life."* Then, without prompting, his eyes closed, as pitch blackness descended.

In total darkness, the man's voice was heard in heightened and emphatic urgency. Jason could smell his breath as he spoke.

In total darkness voices and sounds seemed much clearer, much louder. And there was no longer any doubt; Jason heard metal being hammered.

In total darkness, he had no clue as to what was happening around him. With fear of the unseen growing, Jason desperately wanted his eyes to open. He attempted to stir himself, to forcefully take control of his body. That effort was completely unsuccessful.

After what seemed like an eternity but was more likely only a few seconds, his eyes opened once again. The orange-eyed man, still holding his shoulders, shook him violently and Jason looked upon his traumatized, skeletal face. In the fringes of his view, he saw muscles flexing on the man's arm as he tightened his unfelt grip.

The man moved his taut lips but there was no audible sound out of his mouth. Off in the distance, the horseman with the wetted sword began taking more specific notice of the situation.

Jason thought his time to abide by this man's incomprehensible request was getting short. His vision jerked up then quickly down and his voice yelled something so loud that his ears rung with the vibration. He was quickly released and the man moved on to the next in the group.

His head lowered and his eyes remained open. With only boulders and sand in view, Jason felt like an animal waiting to be slaughtered. Depending solely on his hearing, he knew when all the men tied together had similarly agreed to whatever was said. When the man who had spoken returned to the raised portion of the rocky shore, his head lifted to see the interrogator huddled with the men carrying the whips.

After a brief conversation with the horseback riders, including, to his absolute relief, the murderer with the bloody rapier, another cannon shot off.

Jason saw that the first two rows of tethered men had moved closer to the building. They were being fitted with wide metal wrist and ankle cuffs connected by chains. As he went through the area where the ropes were cut and the cuffs added, Jason yelled out. Hearing his voice express pain without feeling anything advanced the shock of the situation by quantum leaps.

The sound of affixed chains rattling was intriguingly morbid as the group, 14 in all, lumbered towards the building. Following the second cannon shot, that drawbridge had again lowered across the ditch that flanked the building, and again the gate rose. The men once tethered together by rope were now chained individually, allowing them to walk in a single file line.

They were forced to walk up to the drawbridge. As Jason moved forward he saw more men within the compound's walls keeping the group advancing by threatening violence with sticks. While walking across the moat a strong odorous smell rammed his nose from the right side. His head turned to reveal the body of the beaten and impaled man lying in the charnel. The vultures had begun their work.

Once inside the compound, the drawbridge creaked back up, being pulled by a thick, stressed rope and turned onto a large wheel by two men straining with the effort. The portcullis lowered behind it. The chained men were herded to the side, past a door containing one square opening with three linear bars, two of which were clutched by dark, wrinkled black hands.

Skin sagged down from flesh-less forearm bones. There was no face visible. Jason was relieved when the men shuffled past that door.

Relief was brief, for about 40 feet into the compound there was another entrance, this time with an open door. When the men got there, they were forced to enter. As each man stepped up to the entrance they aggressively turned away. The snapping whip motivated them to keep moving through the doorway, chains chinking with every step.

Within the compound's walls, Jason was struck a few times, but not ferociously, as this violence seemed intended for acquiescence rather than to injure. He had not felt the slightest bit of pain, though his body reacted to each blow with quickened steps. Once he reached the entrance to that room he stopped, for now his body and mind were in perfect sync - neither had any desire to go through this doorway into a dark, damp dungeon.

His passive resistance was futile as he was forcibly pushed inside.

Close look at one of El Mina' Vintage Canons

View of Canons pointed out over Atlantic Ocean by Ferris Shelton 1998

El Mina's Rocky Shore by Janice Mazzallo 2018

El Mina's Rocky Shore by Ferris Shelton 1998

Wednesday

The Vision

Chapter 16

Crossing the threshold, Jason's view went dark and his whole body twitched.

He was awake but reluctant to open his eyes yet relieved to feel his backside nestled on his mattress. Was he safe? To be sure, Jason peeked through partially opened eyes to see the furnishings of his bedroom. As the room's details came into focus his mind became freer of confusion. The dream was fresh, especially that last image - the one of the room.

The changeover from sleep to wakefulness was seamless, happening in midbreath – the inhalation as he was pushed into that room; the exhalation arrived with him in near shock lying still in his bed. When he finally fully opened his eyes he was completely awake. He felt as though he had not slept at all – pre-sleep weariness had not diminished one bit.

What the hell was happening?

Rather than relive the dream experience Jason tried to make some sense of it all. The nightmares were stacking on themselves, night after night, with increasing intensity. On this day just last week, he lived a normal, simple life. However, since Sunday, his nights had become a living nightmare. And none of it made sense.

A thunderous rumbling in his stomach made him feel he might vomit. Without moving, Jason worked to suppress the urge by tightening his body - mentally willing the contents in his abdomen to stay put. When he finally relaxed, an all-over chill brought on shivers after another night of heavy sweating. The clock on the nightstand said 4:30 AM; still an hour-and-a-half before the alarm would sound. Callie had moved to the other side of their king-size bed. She was fast asleep, snoring slightly.

Encroaching depression forced him to take the dreams more seriously, considering ever wilder scenarios before stumbling on an odd relationship. It was not the answer; but more a continuation of an absurd thought process. He felt a building pressure to abandon it altogether because it began to border on the ridiculous.

The thought dead-ended. Was it pure folly or somehow plausible? Jason was determined to review his thought's roadmap no matter how illogical it seemed. His thinking was sluggish and scattered as he considered many hypotheses and attempted to find the one that, when properly sorted, might be a blueprint for madness.

Sunday night he dreamed of crashing into the back of a man's head. Monday night he dreamed of dancing and then, the net, as if...Jason swallowed hard. His stomach bubbled. Yes, in that second dream - he was caught by men wielding sticks! He was in the net when he woke up Tuesday morning. And then last night...

Remaining prostrate in the bed, he stifled the growing urge to release the gastric fluid brewing in his abdomen. Employing ever-wilder desperation, he began to fill in the detail of last night's dream. He thought back on the stunning, almost surreal sunrise; the beating of the man and his ultimate murder; and that strange language shouted at him with deadly import.

Beads of perspiration rinsed his forehead, trickling down a face stricken with anxiety. Having no feeling in his body then, the activity going on around him in the dream was real enough to feel in the marrow of his bones now. Trying to get a grip, he shied away from further review, not being sure if he was on the right track or suffering from dementia. He had little confidence in his ability to think clearly.

There was another attempt by his stomach to expel its churning contents and though fought back, his ability to do so was waning. Jason sat upright in bed considering that maybe he was going mad, losing his hold on reality. Or, maybe he was ill, in need of some prescription to free him from these recent problems.

All he absolutely knew was how confused and tired he felt.

His body convulsed with the next surge and the involuntary sounds out of his throat rattled. An acidic taste in his mouth was powerful enough to start him towards the bathroom. He smelled urine as he stood-up. His pajama top was moist with perspiration but the bottoms, the sheets, and an irregular blotch on the mattress were soaked with urine.

Standing to his feet, Jason walked trance-like into the bathroom, bending over the sink only to find the sensation to vomit a false alarm. His heaves were painfully dry.

Eventually, he stood at the mirror staring at eyes stained red by thick blood vessels stretching out from the iris. He felt even worse than he looked.

Taking a cold shower, Jason was careful not to wake the still sleeping Callie. Tiptoeing around the room finding shorts and a T-shirt, he eventually walked downstairs. He went to the kitchen to make a pot of coffee. Though extremely tired, the last thing he wanted to do, even at this early hour, was fall back to sleep.

While filling the coffee pot with water he gazed out the window at the early morning darkness and saw something shining dimly, moving across the sky.

"What is that?" he whispered aloud, looking out at the strange site. It was not a star or streetlight or anything that would logically be along the dark morning horizon. Blinking a number of times, Jason thought the light was getting wider, pulsating into a shape.

He stared intently, looking for any indication of what this thing might be. Looking off to either side for any other similar objects - the light seemed to grab and pull his eyes back.

The coffee pot began to overflow under the running water from the faucet. Distracted, he used his other hand to turn off the tap while very briefly looking away. Tilting his head back towards the window, he was startled to see a white bird sitting on the windowsill.

The water-weighted coffee pot dropped into the metal sink but Jason did not dare take his eyes off the creature perched outside the window screen. The light was gone but the sight of this strange, beautifully shining bird caused blood to rush like white-water river rapids through is veins.

There was a gentleness about its luster. The luminescence affected Jason's attention like a magnet on steel. The bird's brilliance did not allow him to look away or even blink - he was hypnotically captivated.

The glow emanating from the bird steadily increased. Brightness radiating out from the dove-like creature began to optically encroach on, first the window, then the kitchen walls, cabinets and counter tops.

The luxurious white light gave a sense of being surrounded by a scintillating sheen that was not bordered or bound as it blocked out walls, ceiling and floor - yet, left him completely intact. Before long, Jason was standing in whiteness.

The only audible sound was a soft swoosh - as if a person were repeatedly trying to blow out a trick candle. It was gentle and consistent, and manifested itself in a regularly timed cadence.

Transfixed, Jason saw an inscription slowly beginning to take shape in front of him. That swooshing sound accompanied the letters' appearance in perfect coordination while the calligraphic font was large and old-style. Jason read the words, but in his mind heard his voice in a strange tongue.

The message read:

YESHAYAHU

30 26

"The moon will shine like the sun
and sunlight will be seven times brighter,
like the light of seven full days
when the Lord binds up the bruises of his people
and heals the wounds He inflicted."

An amplified, echoing voice repeated over and over:

"Kwan no fefini. Kwan no fefini. Kwan no fefini"

As the words faded, Jason blinked for the first time in minutes. His eyes reopened to find the room back as it was.

"Jason, what's wrong with you? Why you screamin'?"

Callie's presence in the kitchen was a total surprise. He had not heard her come in but her voice was on the verge of hysteria. The sudden change was disorienting and required time to adjust. Jason stood there in a state of semi-shock, trying to reel in his senses.

"What's wrong with you, Jason? Why you actin' like this?" demanded Callie.

Looking baffled, Jason eventually turned to her and asked, "Did you see the bird?"

"What bird? What you talking about? And what is it you shoutin'?"

"Did you see the light?" Jason continued his unsure inquiry, "the bright light?"

"What light? What bird? What are you doing standing in the kitchen screaming like you crazy?" Callie impatiently asked. "And why are the sheets so wet upstairs? Did you pee in the bed?"

He realized she was not aware of what had happened. He was not sure if even he knew what happened. So, there he stood in silent perplexity.

"Jason, you startin' to scare me! What in the world's wrong with you?"

His burdened shoulders slumped. Looking out the window and then back to Callie, tears flushed down his face as he dropped to his knees. Reflexively, she squatted, wrapping him in her arms.

In all their years together she had never seen him cry. She held him close as tears turned into a quivering sob. Callie adjusted her position to allow for his weight and hyperventilating breathing, as he burbled weakly, "Sweetie, I think I'm going crazy. I'm having these bad dreams at night and now..." Pausing, he lifted his head from her chest, before continuing, "And now I... I just had some sort of vision."

"A vision?" Callie asked, bringing him close once more. Over the top of his head she asked, "What kind of vision?"

"I'm not resting when I sleep. It's as if I've been awake straight through the last few nights. It's driving me crazy," cried Jason.

He explained how he must have lost bladder control during the dream. Callie continued asking questions about how he ended up in the kitchen speaking words that weren't English. He had no answer except for the bird and the light, which she refused to accept, so finally he said he did not know.

Rising to his feet, eyes and cheeks moist, Jason knew something had to be done or he risked going stark raving mad.

Chapter 17

Was he hallucinating? The light, the bird, the absolute whiteness could not be real – could it? Of course not! He was standing in his kitchen, not on some special effects movie set. Could lack of sleep over the past few nights cause his mind to start playing tricks on him?

Jason was becoming concerned, so he decided to call his friend, Dr. Kenneth Mendes. They had met at a Super Bowl party a couple of years ago and hit it off so well they decided to golf that next weekend. A strong, positive bond developed between the two men, and they'd been good friends ever since. Mendes, a fair-skinned, slender man with a bit of a quirky, jokester personality could be tough to handle at times.

They were often friendly competitors; whether on the golf course, playing whiffle ball in the backyard, or chess over brandy - to the winner went the spoils and the trash talking. Jason had gotten better at verbally competing but was usually no match for Mendes' quick, intelligent wit. Still he thought Mendes could be a very funny man without being mean-spirited and his humor was often self-deprecating.

Born in Ethiopia to mixed parents, a statuesque African woman and a European-American man who went to Africa with the Peace Corps after college. When they met and began a relationship, Mendes' father considered it a geographical fling, but after the pregnancy and the subsequent birth of Kenneth, his father knew his son's best shot in life was in the United States.

He sent for the mother and child and married her upon their arrival in America.

Kenny Mendes did not acknowledge Ethiopia as a part of his nationality, instead claiming to really be half Eritrean. He said Eritrea was conquered by Ethiopia sometime back but they were fiercely independent and refused to be culturally consumed by their conquerors. Jason used to laugh when Mendes spoke of this. He said it was like him not being a citizen of the United States of America but rather a Georgian or Chicagoan.

Desperately hoping that Kenny could diagnose and correct whatever was wrong, Jason drove into work obsessed by his troubles. Arriving at the Buckhead Building, he entered quickly. Being preoccupied with his thoughts and uncharacteristically silent, he preceded to his office, where he telephoned Mendes right away. After being told Mendes was on another call, Jason left a message for Kenny to call him back as soon as possible.

Renae walked into his office as he hung up the phone. She was wearing a white blouse buttoned to the neck and a long plaid skirt that flapped near her knees as she walked but snuggly hugged her hips and that generous keister. She walked right in and stood at the chair next to his desk.

"Good morning Mr. Scott...I mean...Jason. Is this outfit more appropriate?"

"Renae, I didn't mean the other day that you had to dress like a nun."

"These are my sanctified cousin's old clothes. Ya'll don't pay me enough to buy stuff like this."

"Renae, I don't have time for this kind of..."

"I know Jason, but I just wanted to tell you one thing that I didn't mention Monday. Mr. Farrington liked me until I wouldn't go out with him. I use to get all kinda compliments from him on my shape. Don't you think it strange that now he has you talk to me 'cause he know he can't."

"Renae if you have a complaint about Bob..."

"I ain't got no complaints, Jason. I told you I need this job. But I wanted you to know - and to ask your advice."

"Advice? On what?"

"Should I go out with him to keep my job?"

"I'm not going to sit here and listen to this bullshit!"

"Well I'm sorry, Mr. Scott but the other day you was talkin' to me like you was my brother so I decided to tell you the truth and ask your advice. But I don't mean no disrespect."

"No Renae you weren't, I'm...I'm just tired."

"Yeah, you don't look too good. Are you sick?"

"I don't know. I may be catching a cold. Listen though, I understand the situation better and I will get back to you on that advice. Just not today."

Ring - ring

"Okay, Mr. Scott," Renae walked toward the door while saying, "I wouldn't ask for your advice if I wasn't going to at least consider it."

Ring - ring.

"All right Renae, I'll get back to you, soon." Jason picked the phone in a hurry. "Hello, Edwards Industries, this is Jason."

"Yo Jason how you doin', man?"

It was Kenny Mendes calling back.

"Not good, Kenny. Hold on one minute."

Jason stood, closed the office door and returned to his desk. "Okay I'm back."

"Yeah, so what's wrong with you? Still bruised from that chess board whipping I gave you Saturday night?"

"Yeah, and I need to see you on other matters."

"Well, I'm free this Saturday night as long as you feed me."

"No Kenny, I'm having some real problems, but I don't want to discuss them at work. Can we make an appointment today or tomorrow?"

"You mean a medical problem?"

"I don't know. But, I'm having problems."

"What kind of problems, Jason? Is Callie all right?"

"Yeah, she's fine. It's me. I'm not sleeping very well at night. And, I'm having these weird dreams."

"Did you try having sex with your wife?"

"Kenny, quit fucking around, man. This is real; I think it's psychological more than medical. It could be something that I'm ingesting; maybe it's an allergic reaction. I don't know, but I need to get some answers."

"Well Jason what are your symptoms? This is beginning to sound serious."

"I can't do this now Kenny, don't you have office time available this week?"

"Well, I can make time for you Jason. How about tomorrow morning at nine? Do you think you'll fall dead before then?"

"No, that sounds great. I mean, I've had three dreams in a row, maybe the third one is the charm and there won't be another."

"So... you're dreaming. Is there anything else? Have you had pain or other discomfort?"

"I have a headache and lately an upset stomach, but these are nothing compared to these dreams."

"I mean if it's serious enough I could see you today."

"No, tomorrow is fine. I'm having trouble sleeping and it's been going on for a few days. They're keeping me from resting. But, I don't think it's that urgent."

"I had no idea that schooling your ass on the chess board would cause you these kinds of problems. Would you like me to let you win a couple to give you some positive reinforcement?" Mendes asked playfully.

"Goodbye Kenny, see you tomorrow morning." Jason was in no mood for Kenny's smart-ass comments.

The workday was tough treading. He felt drained and lethargic. Not greeting people in his usual manner that morning prompted a few coworkers to inquire if he was feeling all right.

One of them was Terri McGowan, who suggested he go home, especially after hearing of the doctor's appointment that next morning. He did indeed leave the office early but did not go home.

After the episode that morning, Jason thought being home alone was not such a great idea, so he planned on arriving home after Callie. To fill the time, he went walking downtown.

Occasionally allowing himself to be distracted by one thing or another, he mostly walked - up and down the streets, in and out of stores - figuring if he could get himself physically tired enough, maybe he would get a good night's sleep.

On the way back to his car he spotted a small one-story, natural herb and tea shop named Just Add Honey. It had a café to one side and counter space in front of glass containers on the other. Jason decided to check for an herbal solution.

A unique sounding chime sounded as he opened the door. A woman sat behind the counter.

"I'll be with you in a sec."

"Do you have something to help with sleep?"

"Oh, those items are right over here." She pointed to an area directly behind the counter.

Jason walked over and she stood-up, returning a large container to a shelf but still holding a smaller one.

Without looking in Jason' direction, she pointed to a section of shelves. "My name is Judy. You're having trouble sleeping?"

Judy was a slender African-American woman with dreadlocks down to the small of her back. The locks were mostly black but gray strands worked back from the roots near her temples and forehead. Looking around 40 years-old, she had an earring in her nose and a polite buck-toothed smile.

"I'm not getting restful sleep."

"Well, we have Lavender and Chamomile. But, I think the best is Valerian Root." As she turned to look at Jason, she dropped the container and leaves spilled out on the counter and a few onto his clothes.

Jumping back, Jason frantically wiped at his trousers until he realized the material was dry and falling to the floor. He bent down to address his shoes and pants cuff before stepping away from the debris and looking up. Judy stood frozen. She had not moved to assist in the clean-up or even acknowledged the spill. She seemed in a daze.

Only partially snapping out of it, Judy mumbled, "Umm... sir...I'm uh, so sorry...for...umm."

The door chime sounded again when an older woman entered, "Hi Judy, sorry I'm late." A woman with a slight, thin frame and wearing a brightly colored hair-wrap rushed in.

Judy, having never taken her eyes off Jason said, "Mister, I'm so sorry for this mess. Please, allow me to pay for the Valerian." She called out, "Hi Sophia" to the woman that just entered then turned and whispered to Jason. "She's my shift relief. Let me clean this up and walk out with you."

"That not necessary, I'll just pay for the..."

"No please, sir. I can't talk in the store."

"Is something wrong?" Jason queried.

"No, no, I want to speak with you for a minute, it won't take long. I'll meet you outside with your Valerian, okay? It's on me because of the inconvenience."

"I guess so...but..."

"Fine, I'll get this cleaned up." She turned and walked away.

A bit confused as to what just happened, Jason stepped to the door and Judy joined him soon after.

"What's going on?" Jason asked.

"Sir, that's my question for you?"

"What?"

As they exited the store the closing door cut off the sound of the chimes.

"I'm an empath, sir." Judy handed him a small bag.

"A what?"

"I might be able to help you if you let me"

"Help me with what?"

"Did you drive here? Where is your car?"

"It's down the street at..."

Judy starts walking fast in the direction he pointed with Jason following in tow. "The Valerian can improve sleep quality but it won't solve your problem."

"How do you know that, Judy?"

"It's a superficial remedy. You have deeper problems."

"You don't know my problems."

"Listen carefully, now that I have met you, your situation could affect both of us."

"Judy!" Jason shot back. "There is no us."

Replying with a hollow laugh, "You don't get it, do you?"

"Get what?"

"It's not about me. It's about you. You can't be killed or die while you're sleeping!"

Judy stopped and looked at him without saying a word. After hesitating, with wide-eyes, she gave an exaggerated head nod then stepped away.

"How did you know about...?"

"I'm an empath."

"Judy, what the hell is an empath?"

"I feel other people's energy. I can even take on their emotions. I tend to connect with people in turmoil. You have a troubled mental state and it's not allowing you rest. Isn't that why you're here?"

Much more curious, Jason now walked double time to keep up and hung on her every word as she continued.

"My guess is that you are having a vicarious experience – quite possibly someone else's life – maybe one of your ancestors."

"That's the most ridiculous nonsense I've ever heard."

Judy came to a sudden stop. "Nonsense! You think this is nonsense? Do you have any theories?"

She looked toward the street very impatiently during the silence before returning a sharp look at Jason. "Whatever is going on, you must be careful. Your life is in danger."

"Because I came to your shop looking for sleeping tea, you've determined I'm going to die soon!"

"Are you trying to be funny? Or are you really this confused? You've told me nothing yet you're still walking and talking. Being a 'Doubting Thomas' about everything is wasting valuable time. Time you don't have."

She took off walking even faster. Jason was having trouble keeping up.

"My car is near Hurt Park. Do you need a ride?"

"No, I live locally. I hope you realize this is bigger than sleeping. Or whatever else you may think this is about. The intensity of your emotional state of mind is the strongest I've ever felt."

"Judy, living someone else's life is not reality."

"These problems you are having are real, are they not?" She abruptly paused the quick pace again. "You have made your own reality."

Jason stopped after nearly bumping into her. He stepped back to quietly study Judy for a few seconds. She seemed embarrassed by his stare, stating, "Sir...I...,

"My name is Jason and my car is right there." Stepping around to block her from further racing up the sidewalk, he calmly added, "Judy, dreaming is not reality."

"Mr. Jason, you're being too cavalier with this. Paranormal experiences are not to be trifled with."

"Paranormal! You mean like ghosts or something? Judy I'm not seeing ghosts."

"'Ghosts' isn't really an accurate description. But I'll go with it." Shaking her head slightly, she asked: "Jason, if you're not seeing 'ghosts' then what are they?"

A quick retort wasn't ready. With tightening jaw muscles, Jason thought about the question. Finding no opinion, he meekly offered, "Judy, I need to get home. Sure you don't need a ride?"

"No sir, I'm very comfortable walking. I will pray for you. You need God now. Good luck, Jason."

Jason crossed the street to his car. On his way to the highway he saw Judy walking down the street as fast as some might run.

He arrived home mentally exhausted and physically drained. Opening the front door, Jason smelled the scent of flowers - of azaleas - and saw that a vase of the sweet-smelling blossoms were placed in the foyer. The aroma was fresh and strong. Jason always considered his home a sanctuary - calming, relaxing, and peaceful. Even during this period of high anxiety, he found comfort in being home.

Callie greeted him with a smile as he entered in the kitchen.

"So Mr. Leave-Work-Early, why you coming home so late?"

"Hi Callie, I went for a walk. I have a lot on my mind."

"I know you do, honey. How you doin'?"

"I could be better. I called Kenny and made an appointment for tomorrow morning."

"Good, I'll go with you."

Callie's manner was very casual and she was strangely quiet about the morning ordeal in the kitchen. Jason concluded she must have talked to Kenny Mendes, too. After they ate dinner, which he only picked over, Callie went upstairs and he stayed on the main floor. He told her he was going to sleep downstairs tonight, hoping that the unusual setting, coupled with sitting upright in a chair, would be uncomfortable enough to stir him, as it had done many times before, in the middle of the night. He considered this a defense against another dream.

When he stepped down into the den there was another vase of azaleas. The room was fully imbued with its charmingly sweet scent. Turning on the television, Jason sat through all the news segments and sports highlights he could stand.

Just before 12 the remote control slipped from his hand, his head fell back against the chair and he dozed off to sleep.

Wednesday Night

The Dungeon

Chapter 18

A powerful stench overwhelmed Jason's senses.

Each breath drawn burned as though lit matches were extinguished with a thrust up his nostrils. Desperately seeking relief, Jason' all-consuming desire to turn his head away from the poignant smell was not met with physical motion.

The air was stagnant but there seemed no opportunity for fresh ventilation anywhere nearby. He felt as though he were being smothered – like a putrid pillow was being held over his face - with just enough oxygen getting through to prevent asphyxiation. Every breath more nauseating than the one before.

He was in a large, inhospitable room. The dreariness of it hit quickly, for it was full of people. Proof of inhabitants were the haunting eyes staring out from across the way. Radiant, caramel-colored irises centered in whites nearly aglow generated a distinctly human aura that offered precious little light in a very dark area.

Their pupils were dilated, indistinguishable from the pitch-blackness of the rest of the room. If eyes are windows to the soul; he saw sets of eyes - scores of them, all reflecting souls traumatically impaired. They stretched wide open, as if reliving some horrific incident. Occasional blinking was the only hint of animated life in the whole span of his view.

The eyes were indiscriminately scattered and mystifying in their range; from top to bottom and from side to side. He was directly across from this sea of eyes - none of which were lower than his, yet they stretched as far as he could see. Still, others sat elevated much farther up than seemed possible.

Moreover, the place was as still as a morgue. No one had uttered a word or made a sound. Fear put his listening on heightened alert.

As a pair of eyes blinked, Jason clumsily focused his gaze there, hoping some other aspect of humanity might be revealed. There his attention and yearning for some other semblance of life would stay until the next blink from somewhere else along the wall.

Discomfort crested anew with each breath, the most recent of which nearly sapped away his faculties. Feeling as if his mind might melt from the noxious fumes, Jason teetered on unconsciousness. He waited in anticipation for a few seconds, timing the next breath and then a few more after that.

His mind and eyes began working in concert, allowing him to mentally brace for the intake of the putrid air. Eventually he noticed his head would rise ever so slightly as he inhaled and then settle back down upon release.

The movement could be measured in fractions of an inch; but as the wall of eyes lowered slightly in his sight, Jason prepared for a breath. In this way, he began to better tolerate the suffocating environment of these oppressive confines.

Within a few cycles, his rhythmic breathing committed to routine, he resumed assessing his surroundings. This miserable room extended out of view on both sides. The full extent could not be determined because his head had not turned enough to afford him a direct look. But along the edges, Jason saw a more lit area to one side and bleak, unyielding darkness to the other.

Seeking to scan the full dimensions of either extreme was impossible, as he was unable to concentrate on any particular area, due to his limited eye movement. They would, at one moment, allow an area to be barely seen then, after a blink of those mysterious eyes, that area would no longer be visible. It was an odd feeling. His focus was milliseconds behind his changing sightlines.

His eyes – seemingly of their own volition – continued darting to intercept each blink along the wall where radiant orbs looked to be staring squarely at their own mortality. They suggested past terror and a personal dread of the future. For what future could one really expect with this creepy room as a point of continuum? Jason believed this to be hell, for no place on God's green earth could be so horrible.

There was a blink to the far right, quickly followed by another from that same set. This double-blink was different from others because the eyelids stayed closed longer and opened much slower afterward. When the lids finally lifted, that internal light had faded considerably; a fact that seized Jason's attention as if he somehow sensed a sinister fate had befallen their owner.

An unmistakable coldness took hold of those eyes. Jason scanned around best he could for others with the same hollow reflection. As they continued to blink none lacked the aura of life. His attention no longer responded as earlier, instead, he stayed focused on the one pair of eyes that slowly grew more and more different from all the rest.

A strange desperation for that pair of eyes to blink once more grew from passing fancy to a serious desire, but there they remained, opened and dimming. He spent much time, or so it seemed, on the unrealized hope of seeing the unmoving eyelids adjust even slightly. Suddenly sound broke through what had been, up to that point, absolute silence.

Footsteps traipsing over a sticky floor were heard in the darkness. Jason was on alert to understand their source.

The approaching noise was totally engaging, utterly disrupting his established rhythm of bracing for each breath. The presence of sound had the effect of lifting the veil, enabling the realness of what he was experiencing to pierce his consciousness like a skewer. Catching up with the rhythm of his breathing,

Jason sternly warned himself to be prepared for every breath thereafter - no matter what.

Chapter 19

The footsteps were getting closer. Eventually, a person shuffled by. Out of darkness, a grey, shimmering light outlined the passing, sweaty frame.

It was a male, naked except for thick wrist and ankle cuffs connected by chain. Slowly and involuntarily, Jason' head turned as the man meandered by. Realizing for the first time his view originated from a lower vantage point, Jason still could not tell if he were sitting, squatting, or kneeling. His mid-vision was no higher than the waist of the man walking by.

As he proceeded through an archway, Jason' senses were struck by a shocking trilogy.

The first was visual; there were scores of people in the next section, their misery quietly expressed by a defeated disposition in dreadful surroundings. A narrower arch, deeper within the section, led to a different portion of this dungeon – which was completely devoid of light. The walker continued through to that opening.

The floor pitched downward, angling lower the further back this wretched place extended. The men seemed frozen in time, most not so much as moving a muscle. A light continuous stream of fluid trickled from higher points along the wall and gathered in the center - the low point of the area, and then ran back towards the un-illumed darkness of the next arch.

A small square opening high on the wall of that adjacent section sat framed by a dull gray light. The height of that opening surprised Jason, for it was 25 to 30 feet above the inhabitants - far above any man's reach. Without any visible point of reference anywhere else in this destitute room, it offered hope of an outside world.

That single window allowed a dingy light to enter the structure. The strongest rays went right through to the innermost recesses of this hellish pit, shining directly on a small man wearing a loincloth with a curious set of beads around his neck.

He looked petrified, clutching the necklace and holding imperfectly rounded beads close to his mouth. Squatting low, he rocked slowly but steadily, back and forth - back and forth - back and forth.

His buttocks, extending out from a ragged piece of cloth, sat on the heels of his feet but never made contact with the slimy floor. Though swaying with obvious nervous energy, the man was careful to maintain his balance and not fall back against the grime.

The light highlighted a grim face as lips mouthed words at the rosary. The other hand stroked the beads dangling down, nervously maneuvering individual spheres between trembling fingers.

Jason watched the man rock to and fro. His knees were grotesquely oversized in relation to the leg bones above and below. And his face – a shudder waved through Jason's mind – lacked flesh in the both jowls and cheeks. He was suffering personified...yet right in the middle of overwhelming sympathy, Jason's eyes shifted again.

Fascination with the man's condition had no effect on his own eye movement as he gazed up at that lone window. It was chimneylike as a putrid fog exited. That emission was hot and damp, yet it provided maddening comfort because it indicated the funky air was moving out.

The second shock: there was a dramatic increase in noise. Quiet up to the point of the sticky-floor steps of the walking man, his ears now registered a cavalcade of sound.

There was low-pitch human murmuring, but he was unable to decipher the source - pain or the sheer agony of being consigned to this hellacious underworld. There were moans and groans, barely audible voices in the air. They could have been the exhaustive results of breathing in the stench, yet there was one sound that was recognizable – it was metal chains - and it was clearly identifiable.

Just between the groans and the moans, book-ending the murmurs and the rumblings, was a constant rattling.

The people were very still yet the slightest movement – every breath taken, every scratch of an itch - was accompanied by the soft noise of "chink, chink, chink." The combination of sounds – discernible, audible human misery along with the relentless chinking of metal chains – amounted to a symphony of the macabre.

Having passed through the lit portion, the walking man slowly descended into the darker section. When he disappeared into the shadows, the sound of feet sloshing through thick sludge ricocheted off the walls. Jason wondered what this liquid concoction could be.

The answer to his musing was immediate for he heard an unmistakable sound. When a man stands and urinates, the sound is distinctive whether the expelled fluid is falling in a commode, on grass, or in ankle deep sludge. Within seconds, it became apparent that the man had added to the source of the putrid aroma.

A concentrated, even more pungent reek rushed out into the community area. Jason's olfactory senses were overwhelmed. The man had stirred a mixture of urine and excrement in the back room, unleashing a newer surge of nauseating fumes into the confines.

That event led to the third and final assault to his system; the odors of the room diversified.

He was in an open-air toilet that settled its contents in the rear. The miasmic wave barreling out through the arch nearly gagged him, making each life-sustaining breath even harder to accept. However, in varying degrees, the choking stench had been there all along, but now there were hints of other scents. Up to then, a masculine-musty aroma competed with the noxious fumes for the worst smell imaginable. Now there were times when other smells teased his senses – a welcoming whisper of something different. He could not stop himself wondering from where these odors could be originating. As that query rolled through his mind, his head looked up and his eyes locked back onto the opening on the upper wall.

Earlier he had seen the stifling air exiting through that lone vent and was sure the contents were the toxic vapors from the cesspool in the rear, that and the body heat and exhaled breath from the scores of men inhabiting this house of Hades.

But now something hopeful happened. He saw an inflow.

For the first time that constant emission was repelled and air from out there – Jason thought derisively *'out where?'* – forced its way into this squalid place. Soon the aromatic content of the breeze wafted by - it was the ocean!

This new fact disturbed him deeply. "*Why*," he thought, "*would hell be situated so near the sea*?" The possible topographical configuration of this set-up was beyond his ken. Seashores and beaches are places people go for holiday and vacation. This place allowed for neither rest nor relaxation.

Combined, these three revelations forced an introspective turn. He seemed in the middle of something with dangerous portent.

Where was he? Why was he in this dark and dank environment? And, most of all, how did he get here? Was he chained? He attempted to assess his personal condition to no immediate avail. All mental effort to stimulate body movement was ignored or not received.

Puzzled, he sought to make a determined adjustment, to make this body move. Commands to move his arms to ascertain if they were cuffed were not honored; commands to move his legs to determine if he was sitting or squatting went wanting. While stupefied at his inability to perform basic human movement, his head involuntarily turned to look straightforward - back at the wall of eyes.

Jason resisted this refocus - wanting to maintain sight of that lone opening, where the ocean-scented breeze originated – and, more specifically, where he thought freedom from this place might reside.

Barely visible in the upper reaches of his vision, he could not focus long on that alluring window. The discomfort he felt was mental, as if his sight was behind the eyes of his body – they were independent yet restricted; free yet not in his complete control.

That window, with its tantalizing smell of freedom was just out of reach – physically as well as optically.

His comfortable view settled on the wall in front and the decreasing glow of those eyes that double-blinked earlier. Their whiteness had faded to a point of being nearly monochromatic with the eyeball itself. Nothing changed with the other eyes along the wall as their indiscriminate, random blinking continued.

But Jason had gained perspective - as a group, they represented the bland stare of the living dead.

Jason felt profound sadness. He felt the psychological agony of this place as a nihilistic wave of emotion hit like a tsunami, causing something inside to seek mercy from the pervasive gloom. Overpowered by this intense sentiment, he could not contain his anguish. He attempted to cry out – to beg for help – to seek God's favor in the form of liberty or death – but he had no voice.

Jason's pleas would not have been just for him because the synergism of abused humanity was more than he could stand. This was an instance where misery did not love company. Even with no feeling in his body, there was a tremendous pain in his soul. It was a torment that was not personal but rather a collective pain felt personally.

Temporarily adrift in specious delirium, Jason was pulled back to the reality of his predicament by an excited rattling of chains. Men rushed from the dark unseen direction, shouting short, incomprehensible words and pointing, causing the entire population to scurry.

His head, however, never moved from looking straight forward, seeing a new wave of horror - an increased horror if that were humanly possible - fall over the eyes populating that far wall.

Those sitting low rose up with bodies still not seen. There was a scramble, a cacophony of shuffling feet and chinking chains, sending nervous shockwaves through Jason' mind. The possessors of those sorrowful eyes were moving to the right, joined by many others hurrying through his view.

The exodus did not include the man with the graying eyes as they remained quiet, unblinking, sitting off in the background.

Jason' head turned towards the crowd gathering in the next enclosure. Saddled with chains, the relocating masses were restricted, forcing a sort of order within the chaos.

He saw that the light source shining through that solitary window had changed. Rays that once shone low into the corners of this hellish pit had perceptibly risen up the slimy wall. The man, once squatting low, while holding beads around his neck, was now standing straight up, literally on his tiptoes, in an apparent effort to keep his eye on the light.

There seemed to be urgency in the manner of his quiet chant, as if an end was to be reached before the light set out of his view. He was oblivious to all around him, completely ignoring the gathering crowd.

A door opened with a loud thud. Light burst forth from the dark side, looking to twist in towards the interior, highlighting a mass of humans repelling back from the opening. A rush of new air, not fresh, but not nearly as putrid, swept through, ventilating the area.

Jason concentrated on the newly lit, overcrowded room full of desperate occupants physically struggling against each other as they frantically moved to the side. Pushing and shoving to gain position that measured mere inches, they jostled in front of the man who double-blinked, but he remained motionless.

There he squatted, arms resting on his knees; hands clasped together; fingers tightly intertwined. His skin looked rough and dry. More light also proved his eyes were indeed melding into a solitary dullish color. He was the only man along the far wall that had not moved.

Shouting voices followed the opening of the door, inspiring Jason's head to move once again. Unprompted, he turned to see men of swarthy appearance, swinging sticks with deadly authority.

His vision rose slowly and choppily. The exodus became more rushed. In their haste, a few men disturbed the perfectly still man squatting along the far wall. He tipped over and for one confirming moment the gray-eyed man balanced on one foot before falling back against the wall.

He was stiff with rigor mortis.

Being shoved to one side, Jason fought against the force to look back over his shoulder. His vision shot down abruptly at an angle. He looked to be falling. Unexpectedly, he raised his hands to brace against the man in front. To his incalculable horror, his hands were cuffed and chained.

Back upright, Jason's head immediately turned to look at the dead man awkwardly wedged in the corner. He was positioned in such a way that his face was angled up in direct view.

More aggressively resisting the force of the men piling to the side, with what to Jason seemed to be great effort, he stopped his forward motion. His body stood immovably strong, staring at the wide-open eyes of the deceased man.

It was a dominating sight that controlled Jason' attention in exact harmony with whomever or whatever controlled this body. Because his head, which at times had not come close to cooperating with his wants, was now looking at precisely the place he wanted.

What captivated both mind and body was the wedged man's face. Hypnotically singular in its horror and perverse beauty, there was an undeniable smile on his lips that suggested, in the last few seconds of life, he saw somewhere better than this place.

Jason tried to reconcile the smile with death but that under-standing was elusive. The human rush away from the opened door overwhelmed, and his body gave way a few inches at a time until the gathering crowd completely blocked his view of the dead man.

Eventually his head turned away. With chains rattling all around, he fell in line moving to the rear.

*Entrance to
Courtyard from
Female Dungeon
by Ferris Shelton
1998*

*The Male
Dungeon
by Ferris Shelton
1998*

*Busts of Africans position in the
Male Dungeon at El Mina
by Janice Mazzallo 2018*

Thursday

The Meeting

Chapter 20

Jason' fingers trembled.

Reluctantly, and with much trepidation, he slowly opened his eyes, fearful of where he might be. The initial visuals were of ceiling tiles and a familiar light fixture – comforting but still inconclusive. Lifting his head from the chair, he longed to see his bedroom. But this was not it. Uncertainty caused him to hold his breathe until finally recognizing the furnishings of the den.

Jason' first inhalation was drawn into a body seemingly resistant to taking in life-supporting oxygen. That first taste of air released all the tension as it refreshed him with the sweet fragrance of azaleas. Another dream! A confusing, terrifying fantasy that ravaged his being before emptying him back to the real-world.

The foul stench of his sleep caused him to brace for a breath in anticipation, even though he was awake now. The dream was so uncomfortably real that not only was his mind getting fooled but his body was as well. Unnatural eagerness accompanied the next series of deep, accelerated breaths. Once they began to slow, he looked at the clock on the mantle – it read 5:45. In 15 minutes the alarm would sound upstairs and Callie would be up and about.

Leaning forward, Jason saw the television still on. Not even the flickering picture and uneven sound could wake him from the nightmare - a nightmare that gripped his psyche in a way that was difficult to shake. Instead of rest, Jason felt he had just

experienced a life-threatening thrill ride. They were taking do-
minion over his sleep; each one progressively worse, and now
after a fourth consecutive night he had reason to wonder if they
would ever stop.

Desperately needing a break, Jason felt he'd do anything to
avoid another dream, even if that meant staying awake all night.

The prospect of not sleeping for an entire night was less than
comforting. How long could he function without sleep? The
bitter reality was that he was well on his way to finding out because, though his eyes were closed, there was no rest behind his
eyelids. Unspeakable horror was getting in the way.

Could there be much difference between staying conscious
all night with the attendant adverse effects on his health or falling into a nightmare that was very nearly scaring him to death?

In a dramatic leap of - if not faith, then desperate hope -
Jason remembered today's appointment with Dr. Mendes. This
thought gave him a burst of energy. There was reason to expect
this would be the day his life returned to normal. Or, at the very
least, the dreams would be diagnosed and a remedy found. He
knew of no rational explanation for these intense dreams occurring during restless sleep.

Standing to go upstairs, taking two steps from the chair, he
looked back and stopped in his tracks.

A neat, perfectly outlined blotch of moisture soaked the
fabric. It was sweat, but what struck Jason as particularly odd
was he had not moved at all while sleeping. The moisture patch
was neither smudged nor smeared, but remained only where his
body - arms, butt and legs - were in contact with the chair.

On the top ledge of the chair, where his neck had lain, was a
four-inch column of damp fabric with no wetness to either side.
It represented his presence on the chair as though a part of him
were still there - a damp and darkened shadow remaining in
place.

Seeing so much of his body fluids absorbed into the upholstery made Jason thirsty and he drank three tall glasses of water before going upstairs to prepare for the appointment with Dr. Mendes.

A nervous, mostly quiet morning continued with the drive into the city. Traffic was unusually sparse, moving at a good clip into midtown Atlanta. During the ride, Callie and Jason settled for discussing new building projects seen along the way. This limited interaction was distant, cloaked in the knowledge that both knew something the other did not.

To Jason, Callie appeared on edge, and he desperately wanted to comfort her - to tell her everything would be fine, but he could not know that for sure. More to the point, he did not want to bring up topics they had both so artfully avoided thus far. Callie provided nervous chatter while Jason returned thoughtless, truncated remarks on cue.

For most of the ride, Jason tried to relax in the passenger seat, preoccupied with thinking about sleep - real, restful, regenerative sleep.

After parking in the garage, their walk to the medical center was uncomfortably quiet for two people that know each other so intimately. To break the tension, Jason stepped close, putting his arm around her waist asking, "Honey, how are you holding up?"

"Oh Jason, I'm fine - I'm more worried about you. But I keep tellin' myself that it's just dreams." The words nonchalance did not quite match the concerned tone of voice.

He opened the front door of the Midtown Medical Center, allowing her to walk through, while countering, "Sweetheart, they're more than 'just dreams.'"

Out of Jason's sight, Callie's look turned pensive. That last comment led her to honestly revisit the original question. Of course, she was 'holding up.' She was a strong person – but something was not right – trouble was lurking close-by and she could not quite wrap her mind around it.

Dr. Kenny Mendes was standing at the front desk talking with two nurses. Mendes, seeing Callie and Jason approaching, made a few hasty comments before turning to greet them.

"Ah, Mr. and Mrs. Scott, how are you this morning?"

"Why Dr. Mendes," Callie politely smiled, "you're so formal this morning. We're good."

Becoming a bit anxious, Jason spoke a simple, strained greeting, "Hi Kenny. How ya doin?"

"Fine, my friend," responded Kenny, putting his hand on Jason's shoulder, "Listen, I got you all set up, but we have a tight schedule today. So Callie, if you will have a seat in the waiting room, Jason and I will go over for the CAT scan and..."

"CAT scan!" exclaimed Jason, much more animated. "Kenny, I just had a physical in March."

"That's great," Mendes shot back. "Who did the physical?"

"My primary care physician, you know, Doctor..." Jason hesitated; his doctor had a difficult name to pronounce.

"But you didn't call him did you? You called me. So I have to prove to myself that you're still alive," Mendes interjected, waving his index finger.

Jason hated the thought of a full physical. He did not think it dealt directly with the dreams, and that was the reason he was there. The look on his face fully expressed that sentiment.

"Kenny, I don't need a physical," sounded Jason defiantly, mustering a stronger tone. "It's a waste of time. I can tell you what's going on with me."

"Listen Jason, with what I know now," said Mendes sternly, "we need to systematically eliminate all physical conditions associated with night sweats and aggressive movement in your sleep."

He hadn't told Mendes that. Jason glanced at Callie but she belatedly averted her eyes, leaving him to return his attention to

Mendes, who continued. "You're also having traumatic visions and chanting - no, pardon me, yelling! - some incomprehensible phrase. And you recently developed a bladder problem while sleeping."

Jason sought eye contact with Callie again. She was not taken by surprise this time and was already looking away. Mendes checked his watch before adding, "As a doctor, but more importantly as your friend, I'm telling you that you're going to have this physical, if not for yourself, then for Callie. Why didn't you tell me this stuff was happening to you?"

Once again, Jason glanced at Callie. This time she was staring right back at him.

Mendes concluded, "So, my friend, don't tell me about wasting time or not needing a complete exam. Look at you! I'll bet you've lost 10 pounds - you look terrible. And your wife is seriously concerned about you. Listen, we don't have a lot of time to waste. Your CAT scan is scheduled for nine o'clock and we're already late. We have a lot to accomplish this morning because at two o'clock there's a psychologist coming in to talk to you. You can tell us 'verbally' what's going on then. In the meantime, I have to make sure you are okay 'medically.' So, are you coming voluntarily, or do I have to get a couple of male orderlies to strap you to a gurney? At this point, I can make a call and limit your options," Mendes said as he grabbed a radio from his hip.

"No Doctor Mendes, that won't be necessary," mumbled a still reluctant Jason. "Lead the way."

"Alrighty then." Mendes smiled and said, "Now, Callie have a seat. I'll be back to talk to you once I've gotten the process started."

Looking at Jason, Callie's eyes glistened. He whispered, "I love you, honey. Everything will be okay." Kissing her gently, he then squeezed her hand harder than he intended to. Dr. Mendes grabbed Jason's upper arm and led him towards the set of double doors that was the main entrance to the medical center.

"Let's go, chief. If you behave yourself, I'll have one of the nurses give you a lollipop when we're done."

Jason went through the double doors thinking Kenny Mendes was a jerk and also knowing that he was one of his truest and best friends. With each step, his confidence grew that everything possible would be done to find a solution for the problems he was experiencing.

The physical examination lasted over three hours.

Chapter 21

Electrodes glued and taped to his body and head connected to machines that beeped and droned on endlessly. Jason was poked and prodded over much of his body. They took stool, blood, urine and, saliva samples, and for some reasons they wanted a very painful culture from his eye fluids that hurt like hell.

By the end, with his stress level even higher than before, Jason was exhausted. Returning to Kenny Mendes' office around 12:15, he found Callie sitting, reading a magazine. Jason told her all about the physical examination but detected a disinterest because she never looked directly at him.

Her eyes shifted from down and away during most of his explanation to up and away when she thought he'd concluded. Obviously, something else was on her mind so he cut short the story and silently waited for her to offer a topic. After a few moments, she shifted close to his side.

"Kenny is making his rounds but he'll be back when the psychologist, a Doctor Howard Caswell, arrives"

"Okay, thanks. So, why are you so...?

"Are you hungry?" blurted Callie, "Because I'm going to go to the cafeteria and get lunch."

"No Honey, I mean, I'm a little hungry but more tired. I don't want anything. I think I'll try to get some rest."

"You should eat, Jason! What are you tryin' to do, starve yourself to death?" Callie was nearly shouting.

"Of course not, honey. What's wrong with you?"

"I don't know...I'm just...Jason, I don't know," she whispered, her adjusted deportment failing to mask whatever was bothering her. "It's nothing really. Okay, I'll be back."

She left the office without looking his way again. He believed her to be concerned because he now knew she had spoken to Kenny independently but had not told him this. "What a great wife," he thought. She's probably feeling bad because she thinks she may have been disloyal to him.

Stretching out on a leather couch in Kenny's office, Jason felt himself becoming energized emotionally over the upcoming opportunity to describe the dreams and the prospect of finding some way to end them. That comfort settled in as he closed his eyes and thought how nice it would be to get just a little rest. In no time he was off to sleep.

He awoke to see Kenny standing behind his desk and another man sitting off to the side. Callie was back, sitting on the end of the sofa where he slept. Coming to, he wisecracked, "Good morning."

"Well Sleepy, how do ya feel?" Mendes asked.

"A little better," Jason responded. "How long have I been sleeping?"

"When I got back to the office at 1:30 you were out like a light," Mendes said while taking a seat, "Callie was here finishing lunch and Dr. Caswell arrived 10 or 15 minutes later. We've been here talking for another 15 or so. Oh, I'm sorry Jason, this is Dr. Howard Caswell, Director of Psychology at Grady Hospital. Dr. Caswell, this is the dreamer, Jason Scott."

Jason and the psychologist exchanged cordial greetings. Caswell was a big man, maybe 6'2" or 6'3", and was thick with broad shoulders and a wide, rotund torso. He looked to be about 50, with gray strands of hair sprinkled liberally throughout his head and full beard.

Dr. Caswell had earned the reputation of a maverick in the field of psychology. Though an accomplished man with over 20 years of practical experience, there were times when he was not beyond breaking from conventional doctrine. His experience had taught him that every personal malady did not fit neatly within Freudian or Jungian boundaries - that indeed some disorders were beyond man's ability to categorize, label, and define.

Mendes stood from his desk, poured a cup of coffee and explained what would be happening while the dreams were being discussed. He said the session would be recorded and since this was a multi-dream interpretation, they would need to break after each recap of a dream to allow for questioning from Caswell and himself to fill in any unclear areas.

Finally, Mendes cautioned Jason to be loyal to the true essence of the dreams and to be careful not to falsely elaborate - that "I don't know" is a perfectly good answer if it is indeed true. He warned not to unduly embellish the dreams for it could skew analysis away from a meaningful diagnosis.

After offering coffee to all, Mendes asked if there were any questions. Jason had none, but Callie, having moved in close to him on the couch, was fidgety.

"Kenny, why is the meeting being recorded?" inquired Callie, then revealingly cutting her eyes in the direction of Dr. Caswell.

She had unintentionally taken on a suspicious posture. One predicated not on anything specific but rather on wanting to insulate the man she loved from some unforeseen trouble. Trusting Mendes explicitly, yet not being exactly aware of what the subject matter might be, she was unsure of Dr. Caswell, a total stranger, being in the room.

Mendes took charge immediately.

"Listen, if you are uncomfortable with the recorder we will not use it. But Callie, I strongly recommend we record the telling of these dreams. From what you have told me, what is happening to Jason is abnormal. Still, it is your decision."

Callie lowered her eyes and seemed to whisper something briefly. After a few seconds she turned to look at Jason.

"It really doesn't matter, Sweetie," he said without much interest.

Still unsure, she looked up at Mendes. He smiled and nodded. "Okay."

Mendes depressed the 'Record' button on the recorder and spoke aloud the names of the attendees, the date, and finally the time - it was 2:45.

Jason detailed the first dream. His memory was vivid, but conveying it now to others was very difficult. He told of the flight above the clouds without a plane. He described how peaceful and serene the dream was at first and how he eventually entered a spiraling whirlpool of a hole in the clouds, then finally how he was just about to crash into a man's head before awakening Monday morning.

Afterwards Jason apologized for his inability to verbalize the depth and realness of the dream.

"Recanting a dream is difficult," Dr. Caswell sympathized, "The interpretation is most times shallow and flat, while to the dreamer the actual experience is very powerful. So tell us the best you can, Mr. Scott, with the understanding that the intensity and deep effect is quite impossible to re-create through mere words. But I have one question: Did anything happen Sunday that might trigger the dream?"

Jason and Callie looked at each other.

"We had an argument - no really a disagreement, coming home from a party Sunday night," Jason offered off-handedly.

"An argument about what?" asked Caswell.

"It was no big deal," responded Jason defensively.

Caswell put his pen down and said, "You don't know that Mr. Scott. What was the argument about? Money? Sex? Did something happen at the party?"

Exasperated, Jason said, "It was a personal matter, it had nothing to do with the dreams."

"Well Mr. Scott, if you've already analyzed the dreams, why am I here?" Caswell declared. "A specific event may have triggered the suddenness of these dreams. You can't arbitrarily dismiss something because it's personal. Mrs. Scott, how would you categorize your marriage - good, bad or in between."

Jason sat up on the couch, "Hey, wait a minute Dr. Caswell, what the hell does that have to do with anything!"

"It may have everything or nothing to do with the dreams. But what I'm looking for here, Mr. Scott, is context," Caswell calmly stated. "Out of context, anything in these dreams you've been experiencing can symbolize anything. However, it is the context of the dream experience as provided by the personal association of the dreamer that makes for accurate analysis and possible solutions."

Increasingly annoyed, Jason considered a number of ways to logically rebut what Caswell said. He had not expected a probe into his personal life. After a few seconds of silence, Caswell resumed, "So, how is your marriage Mr. Scott?"

"Our marriage is strong," responded Jason. "We have issues just as any married couple, but nothing too serious."

Dr. Caswell looked over at Callie.

"Our marriage is good," Callie asserted. "I love my husband and I know he loves me."

"And the argument?" Caswell persisted.

"I get a little upset with Jason," Callie quickly conveyed, "because I think he tries too hard to impress his bosses and co-workers."

Jason added, "And I got mad because I feel I know best how to manage my career."

"So, this really isn't a big deal between the two of you?" Caswell asked, turning back to look at Jason.

"No," Jason and Callie said in unison.

After taking a few notes, Dr. Caswell asked Jason to continue with the second dream. However, Jason was beginning to dislike Caswell, thinking he was coming across as an arrogant intellectual. Plus, he had a smug look on his face, as if he viewed the entire session from a lofty, judgmental perch. That feeling was temporarily put aside as Jason recapped the second dream.

He told of the drum recital and people dancing in merry celebration. Recollecting how flaming torches were the only light in a pitch-dark area, he mentioned that all the dancers were black and scantily clad, but ornamented with expensive looking gold jewelry. While telling of the lofted net falling and ensnaring him, and of speaking in a strange, unrecognizable tongue, he stared out blankly at nothing in particular and felt his body temperature rise.

When he finished with the second dream, Jason again felt he had inadequately expressed what had been a deeply intense experience.

Dr. Caswell made a series of notes after which he stated, "Many people tell of dreaming and speaking in a foreign language and it's usually a language they either know or have been exposed to."

Looking up from his pad he stopped writing and asked, "Mr. Scott, do you know any foreign languages?"

"No, not really," replied Jason. His voice barely concealing a heightened aversion for the psychologist. "I studied French at school, but I have not held on to it."

"Was the language used in the dream French?" asked Caswell.

"If the language was French, I would have said so," was Jason's rapid-fire response.

"Okay, Mr. Scott, so what language was it?"

"If I knew that, why would you be here?"

Caswell leaned back in his chair, looked directly at Jason and said, "Mr. Scott, I'm not like Daniel of the Bible, able to pull the dream out of the dreamer while grasping its deeper meaning.

I'm forced to depend on you, the dreamer, for information. You see Mr. Scott, there is a primacy - an exclusivity, if you will - of the dreamer and the dream. Without you being forthcoming, in all aspects, I am limited in the assistance I can provide."

"He's right, Jason," Mendes cut in. "We're all trying to help you."

Jason did not respond, instead he attempted to mentally corral his growing disdain for Dr. Caswell.

"Did you know the language used in the dream?" Caswell asked again.

"No I didn't, Dr. Caswell," responded Jason, still annoyed but beginning to let it go. "It was completely foreign to me."

"Please, Mr. Scott, we don't need you to get defensive," requested Caswell, reaching to grab his pen. "Is there anything else?"

"Well Dr. Caswell, there was something else about the dream that night," Callie offered. "Jason kicked his legs and swung his arms wildly in his sleep."

This comment seemed to interest Caswell greatly as he asked, "Mr. Scott, do you know why you may have been thrashing about in your sleep?"

"Yeah," Jason remembered. "Earlier in the dream, I was dancing to the music."

"You were dancing?" Mendes asked.

"Yes, in the dream, I was dancing," said Jason, who then added, "at least my body was dancing."

"This is very unusual," interjected Caswell. "During dream sleep or REM sleep, the body is usually subject to internal paralysis. It's called 'sleep paralysis' and it in effect keeps one from acting out what they are dreaming."

Scribbling quickly, Dr. Caswell made a series of notes in his pad before asking Jason to continue with the next dream.

Consciously looking for words to convey his personal turmoil, Jason told of walking along a beach tied by rope to other men.

He described the fortress-like structure with old-fashioned cannons that stood as a backdrop to the murder he witnessed of one of the roped men.

It had been so graphically violent that his voice quivered while recalling the specifics of the beating. He commented extensively on the man questioning him in an unrecognizable language. He recounted entering the walls of a huge compound and being led to the most horrible room imaginable. He emphasized that he could hear, see and smell but could not feel a thing in any of the dreams.

"Mr. Scott, you are telling a fantastic story." Dr. Caswell said, "The fact that you cannot feel anything in your dreams is not that unusual. And the fact that you are smelling and hearing in the dream is normal." He paused briefly before adding, "Do you fear death, Mr. Scott?"

"No, not especially," Jason replied. "Although I'm not looking forward to the day. Why do you ask?"

"Many times friends or relatives who have passed on are dreamt to still be alive," Caswell said while spreading his arms, palms up, as if inviting more information. "Did you recognize the man murdered in the dream?"

"No, no I did not." Jason replied, looking as if he wished he had a better answer.

"Dreams often speak to our most troubling, conflict-filled concerns and offer us guidance, inspiration, even hope. That is why some people consider dreams to be religious or spiritual in nature." Caswell added, "Are you deeply concerned about something, Mr. Scott, maybe your own mortality?"

Jason looked at Callie and Kenny before replying, "Dr. Caswell, I can honestly say I am no more concerned about my mortality this week than I was last year, last month, or last week. My only concerns right now are these dreams and what they are doing to me."

"Mr. Scott, these kinds of things don't just start willy-nilly," stated Dr. Caswell, pointedly. "Something caused this to come up for you. This phenomenon appearing randomly is highly unlikely. You need to understand this."

"That may be true, doctor," snapped Jason, with a glare returning to what was a compliant stare. "But what I do understand is that these dreams are ruining my life. Maybe after they stop and I get a good night's sleep we can delve into their origins."

"It may not work that way, Mr. Scott. Treating the effect might not do a thing for you. We may need to find the cause." Grabbing his pad with a look of 'let's get back to the point', Caswell dismissively asked, "Anyway, what about the fourth dream?"

"Before we go there, I need to check on a couple on patients and I think we all could use a break," Mendes said, sensing Jason and the doctor were getting frustrated again. "It's after four, let's take 15 minutes."

Mendes stopped the recorder and with that, he and Dr. Caswell left the office.

As the door closed upon their exit, Callie asked, "Jason, this thing started Sunday night? Why didn't you tell me that?"

"It was just a dream," Jason casually replied. "I really thought nothing of it."

"But you said you thought the dreams are connected."

"I began believing that today."

"Why didn't you tell me that?" Callie voice expressed an annoyance that Jason did not fully understand.

"Well honey, we weren't really talking and you didn't ask…"

"Ask!" a now clearly agitated Callie exclaimed. "Am I supposed to ask if you've been dreaming?"

"Hey, why are you so angry? I didn't want to alarm you unnecessarily and I was hoping it was a one-time thing, that maybe it would just go away," he replied defensively.

"Jason, this is serious! You should have told me, whether you thought they would go away or not." Her words were forceful, much more than the situation warranted in Jason's estimation. Not knowing how to respond, he accepted the scolding quietly.

Finally calming down, Callie asked how he was feeling, her voice a bit kinder, but not much warmer. Jason said the nap helped him greatly - it was the first rest he had gotten all week and he was encouraged to have slept and not dreamed.

Chapter 22

Mendes and Caswell returned to the office a short time later and the recording session resumed. As Jason was about to begin the fourth dream, Callie stopped him, abruptly saying, "Don't forget about Wednesday morning."

"Oh, that's right," Jason remembered. "When I awoke from the dream of being on the beach, I had some kind of vision."

"In the waking hours?" Caswell asked, almost disbelievingly.

"Well, yeah," stated Jason, looking a bit more puzzled as if having to dig deep for this information. "I woke up early that morning and went downstairs to watch television. While standing at the sink making coffee, I saw a bird on the windowsill that looked like the bird I saw Sunday night."

"Wait a minute, Mr. Scott," Caswell interrupted. "What bird Sunday night?"

"Well, Callie and I were not speaking at the time, so I decided to sleep on the porch. Before turning in, I went out in the back yard and a white bird swooped down, it almost flew right into me it was flying so low. It landed on the porch and just sat there for a while. Eventually, it flew away and I didn't think any more about it," said Jason, in a much more thoughtful voice.

For the first time, Jason connected the events of Sunday night and Wednesday morning with the dreams.

This revelation caused Dr. Caswell's demeanor to change dramatically. With an astonished look, he inquired of Jason, "Are you telling me that a white bird visited you on Sunday night before the first dream and then came back Wednesday?"

Jason nodded his head while stating, "Yeah, I guess that's what happened."

"And when I asked you about a trigger or some circumstance that may have hinted at this thing, the bird didn't come to mind?" demanded Caswell.

"I hadn't thought much about either. Sunday was a bizarre coincidence and I figured Wednesday was due to a lack of sleep," Jason said before adding, "As part of the vision not only was there a bird, but also a message. Strange writing took shape in front of me."

"Well, I can't really see why you wouldn't think this was important," Caswell declared, "What did it read?"

"I don't remember," Jason finally confessed, after taking a few seconds to search his mind. "It all happened so fast. I can remember at the top of the inscription there was a word that I didn't understand and numbers above it."

There was a pause as Jason thought back, trying to remember a portion of the inscription.

"This is the story that Callie told me and the reason I asked you to get involved, Dr. Caswell," Mendes said. "It was at this time that Callie heard him shouting in a strange language."

Dr. Caswell turned to her. "Do you remember what he was saying that morning, Callie?"

"It sounded different," Callie replied, "it wasn't Spanish or anything like that. It sounded like, if you will excuse the way I say it, 'Qua no fe-fini' and he was saying it over and over and over again."

Dr. Caswell made more notes. "Jason, what is this language you were speaking?"

Still in deep thought, he slowly muttered, "I already told you, I don't know."

"You said you didn't know the language of a dream, Jason," offered Caswell, "This you were speaking in a wakeful state."

"Y-E-S H-A-Y A-H-U," Jason nearly shouted; spelling out the letters, in a series of threes. "Those were the letters. And the numbers were 30 and 26."

Dr. Caswell made a long page of notes, flipping to a new page he looked up and asked, "Jason, are you sure of the spelling?"

"Not one-hundred percent, but I'm pretty sure," he responded.

"But you don't remember any other part of the inscription?" asked Mendes. "Was it in English, Jason?"

"Yes, it was all English," answered Jason. "I'm sorry, but I don't remember what it read. I paid more attention to the word on top because I didn't recognize it."

"All right, what else?" asked Caswell, now with deep lines creasing his brow. "What about the dream last night?"

Jason began the fourth dream by telling of being in a room that must have been in hell. He tried to convey the overwhelming stench in the air that nearly knocked him out. But how does one express with words such a horrid smell? He mentioned the gloomy atmosphere, the room full of men and the corpse whose eyes were open, reflecting death.

Ending by taking time to explain that the intensity of each succeeding dream increased in magnitude, Jason knew he had not come close to capturing the terror of that awful room.

When he finished, Caswell stood and walked to the corner of the office, all the while leafing through his notebook. Standing at the window for a moment, his mannerism was that of a man about to unveil some very bad news. He retook his seat.

"Jason, you have an unusual problem on your hands. One that is very serious. I could give you a lot of psychobabble by listing plausible disorders or syndromes, but there is no need to start off by heading down a wrong path. What you have described tells me you are in a situation that you have gotten yourself into and only you can get yourself out of. We have spent a good part of the day trying to get behind the dreams as if they were a façade concealing some true meaning. But Jason, the dreams you're having aren't there to conceal - they're there to enlighten."

"Enlighten what, Doctor? What exactly are you saying?" asked a confused Jason.

"I'm saying, your somnambulating act violates sleeping rules and, for that matter, dreaming rules. You are not only moving in your sleep, but dancing," Caswell sharply responded. He never took his eyes off Jason while putting his notebook in the briefcase.

"The activities in these dreams suggest they are lasting a while. Your mind may not be resting - never cycling through an at-rest period. This is sleep deprivation that the body and mind would not ordinarily impose on itself. The connection of the dreams and their building intensity tells me that this is not REM fantasy fare which can be addressed with therapy or medication."

"All right, Dr. Caswell," Mendes chimed in. "I think we all recognize the seriousness of this matter."

"I'm afraid you really don't understand yet," Caswell charged. "Turn the recorder off, if you don't mind. I'll be leaving shortly."

Mendes reached over, pushing the stop button.

"Thank you, Kenny," Caswell said. He turned to Jason immediately, as if free from the restriction of the recorder. "Jason, this is not clinical advice I'm giving you here, but if you don't learn the lesson from these dreams they won't stop until you are well past insane. You see Jason, you are out of balance. There is something called a human trinity in us all. It consists of the mind, the heart, and the soul.

"Most people manage to keep these in a state of equilibrium; however your mind, heart, and soul are in conflict. And, your spirit is trying to get the three back into proper alignment.

So, you see Jason, it is you and only you that can recover this internal balance."

Caswell looked at his watch and grabbed his briefcase. As if an afterthought belatedly came to mind, he added, "Let me caution you Jason. As I have said, this is a very serious problem. You need to figure it out fast because your mind and your body won't stand the strain indefinitely. Going mad is just one of a number of possibilities if you don't find that balance soon."

That conclusion, followed by 15 to 20 seconds of silence, convinced Caswell that it was time. "Now, I must be going. Nice meeting you Callie. Jason, I wish you Godspeed. Ah, Dr. Mendes, will you..."

"Oh yes, Dr. Caswell," Mendes offered. "I will copy the tape and mail it to you within a week."

"Very well, sir." With that, Dr. Caswell left the office.

It was almost six o'clock and the sound of snarling Atlanta traffic served as the background for an uncomfortably quiet time in the office. Looking through papers in a folder, Mendes finally offered, "Well my friend, this is where we are. Your vitals are weakening but still in the normal range; your blood count is okay if a little low and your heart rate is good though your entire system seems to be laboring. If I had to give you a diagnosis right now, it would be physical exhaustion. Ordinarily, I would prescribe sleeping pills and a week away from work, but that does not seem appropriate here."

"Well Kenny, what can be done about the dreams?" Jason asked.

"You were right Jason, your problem is not medical - yet," Mendes said raising his head from the paperwork. "But I will say this; you should not dismiss Dr. Caswell's on and off the record comments."

Mendes closed the papers in the folder, leaned back in his chair, then carefully continued.

"I've visited Africa many times with doctor groups, and there are buildings on the coast that kind of fit the description you have given. They are dotted along Africa's latitudinal coastline. They came to be called slave castles."

"Kenny, it's been a long day." Jason replied wearily. "I can't deal with this. It's too much – dreaming about a castle, for God's sake." Hunching his shoulders while shaking his head side to side, he put physical emphasis on the disbelieving look on his face.

"I know Jason," Mendes said almost apologetically. "But the entire situation is abnormal."

Jason was disappointed and dejected. He hoped this meeting might provide a more reasonable hypothesis.

"So Kenny, what can we do?" inquired Callie.

"Well Callie, we could keep him here and evaluate him overnight," Mendes said.

"No way," Jason stated. "The last thing I want to do is wake up from one of those dreams in a hospital."

"That's fine, Jason," Kenny said, "but it doesn't end here. If that phrase that Callie remembered you saying or the word you spelled is truly from an African language, I'll find it. In the meantime, if you need a sedative, I will prescribe one for you."

"No thanks, Kenny. The nap I took was dream-free so perhaps it's already over," said Jason. He stood to leave.

"Are you sure you wouldn't prefer the medicine, Jason?" asked Callie grabbing for his hand.

"If I had insomnia, that would be a fix, but I have no trouble falling asleep, honey," returned Jason.

"That's right Jason, sleeping pills probably won't help you," agreed Mendes, "but let's take what we have and work with it. I'll make some calls tonight and check with you in the morning."

With that Callie and Jason said goodbye and left the office. During the ride back to Stone Mountain, Callie drove with

Jason sitting in the passenger seat, reclined back, eyes closed, contemplating the past few hours.

Jason considered what Dr. Caswell claimed might be happening. He had to admit that the dreams *were* connected and when the vision and the bird were factored in the entire ordeal took on a different feel.

Earlier in the day Jason dreaded the thought of having another dream. However, now he thought if it did indeed happen, it might answer many questions. With that new information as his driving force, he sought the inner fortitude to face another one.

Ready or not, the possibility of a dream tonight was real, bothersome, and probably unavoidable. Bravery is something one has before going to battle, but once there, mortal fear takes over as self-preservation kicks in. Jason thought, "that's not something you can do in your sleep."

When they got home, Callie and Jason made love with more energy than they had in recent months. Alongside the hungry kisses and electric caresses was an element of trepidation in their desire for each other. Unspoken, but in the back of both their minds, was concern for the immediate future and it heightened both their passions.

Jason was awake for more than an hour after Callie fell asleep, comforted and conflicted by the depth of his love for her. He was tormented by not just what may await him in his sleep but also for what would become of her should something happen to him. With heavy eyes and his nightstand lamp casting its dim, shaded light, he took a deep breath.

Leaning over to kiss Callie's cheek while she slept, he plumped his pillow, and found a comfortable position on his side.

Thursday Night

The Courtyard

Chapter 23

A thousand watts of light flashed from total darkness.

Though his eyes were wide open, seemingly already accustomed to the brightness, Jason's view was snow white. His vision cleared from the outer areas to the center, sharpening much like finely calibrated binoculars. He and a group of men were standing to one side of a large structure. Other people gathered on the opposite side. The two groups looked as if they were lined up formally.

Slowly, the reduced glare allowed details of a large, imposing building to come into view. There were three arched openings in the shade at ground level. They sat underneath a deck extending out from the level above. There, a picketed rail banister lined the overhang and was accessed by inward-curved, spiral staircases running up each side.

Two men walked up each staircase, taking an elevated position on the area. Standing like sentries at attention, they kept a watchful eye.

Another staircase, with two thin, decorative columns on top of newel posts, sat centered on that upper-deck, this one leading to a third level. Large, glassless, window-like openings sat off to either side of a closed door. That door was ornamented with a bizarre, medieval looking coat of arms.

Above that was a long dorm, spanning the entire width of the building. There were a series of small, square cutouts extending from one end to the other. All were blocked from the inside except the one in the middle, which was free of obstructions and wider than the rest.

Palm trees swayed in the breeze above a wall stretching out on both ends of the building. The wall cornered and extended back out of sight. Jason suspected it connected behind him, enclosing a courtyard.

Smoke rose from an obstructed area at ground level; he could not tell from where it was coming.

An obscenely loud bell sounded from on high. It was coming from the center opening on the fourth level. The echoing reminded him of church bells, causing him to wonder what distinguished them from other bells. Did they ring on the hour, or after a service? He couldn't remember.

The ringing bell stilled Jason's mind and he began paying closer attention to the actions in his immediate surroundings. The first ring startled him, interrupting complete silence. The following ones found him adjusting to the shocking reverberations.

Counting the next as four by assuming he missed the first three, he noted increased activity. The calm, still yard livened up with the ringing bell as people began scurrying about.

Five rings. Men had spilled out of the third level opening, racing down the stairs. Once on the landing, some of the men ran down the staircase on the right to get to ground level, mobilizing on the other side of the courtyard. *Six rings.* Jason could not make out what they were doing, for they were a good distance away. However, gray smoke rose skyward in the background.

Seven rings. Most of the men rushing out took the staircase nearest to where he stood. Some of them gathered near the corner as heat vapors distorted the visibility of the area above. *Eight rings.* Jason began taking note of the people around him. The man in front was naked except for wrist and ankle cuffs linked by chain.

Nine rings. Both of the man's ears were oddly mutilated and almost identically scarred.

Ten rings. His earlobes were abnormally stretched down and split up the middle, resembling the forked tongue of a snake.

Eleven rings. Everyone around him sweated profusely. *Twelve rings.* He heard the sweep of waves on a shore not far away.

He anticipated a 13th ring and when that did not happen Jason thought, "Is it noon, or did the bell mean something else?" The ringing had become comforting, allowing his mind to focus on the counting. Without the noise an inexplicable panic swelled within. He had no basis – no clue - as to why a sense of immediate danger had fallen upon him so completely.

Despondency swept in when he heard men talking in that corner generating the smoke. He couldn't substantiate it, but there was real fear that his mortal soul was in jeopardy. That emotional tide controlled his thoughts; not one inch of his mind was free from its prevailing seriousness. It was a feeling that was real - right here - right now.

Horse hooves clacked. Jason mentally tensed as a mounted steed casually walked by. Not until the horse came into view did his head belatedly turn to look directly at the rider. He was shocked by his slow reaction to the sound of approaching danger. The horseman strolled past and dismounted.

The men standing around him looked odd; most wore sheaths of cloth around their waists although some were naked and all were topless. They were lean, muscles rippling and hair clumped, styled, or otherwise arranged in unfamiliar ways.

The men at the very front of the single file line took short, hesitant steps forward. Their movement had no effect on his position; he remained still even as the tethering chain became taut.

A man's stuttered yell blasted through the escalating tension like a rocket headed for the heavens. A sudden vibration was followed by increased tension on the connecting chain. Jason took two short, shuffling steps forward. Moments later, another scream, this one of longer duration, sounding as if it contained two phases.

The first seemed anticipatory; a calm voice rising in volume before expanding to an uncontrolled expression of pure pain. Between the two screams was a sizzling sound, similar to raw meat being placed on a hot grill.

In quick succession the chain vibrated and tensed again. Jason began to pay closer attention to these actions. The next scream was muted, deeper. Where the previous two cries were that of younger men, the latest was apparently that of a mature man. Silence followed.

Heightened awareness led Jason to notice something entirely different. The ever-present ocean smell had occasionally been joined by burning carbons. But something was slightly different now.

It was a new smell, sharp and unavoidable. As he searched his memory to find some comparable smell for this unpleasant odor, he felt the tension of the tethering chain release and three men - naked all - walked away from the corner.

Jason saw them to be in obvious discomfort. Suddenly, another more distant scream from the right side echoed across the compound. It was a female voice. Jason was captivated by the shrill cry for he had not seen any women in the compound.

He was forced to move forward even as he sought a visual for the feminine scream. It was as if his body was on automatic pilot, yet there was no doubt his consciousness was a passenger and not in the cockpit. Jason stepped forward another two steps with the other men in the linear formation. Chain links rattled all around. The sound resembled a tambourine shaken by a person without rhythm.

The movement distracted Jason from understanding the goings on across the yard. The three men who had stepped away from the hidden corner were positioned in the center of the courtyard. His head turned, following their movement. This directional shift allowed a clear view, out past the men, at the far side of the courtyard.

He stared in utter amazement.

Chapter 24

Prior to the bell ringing, Jason noticed people standing in front of that perimeter wall on the other side, but the sun's glare prevented him from seeing clearly. His view was much better now. There were women – all butt-naked - lining the far wall. A filmy residue covered their feet, and their skin was blotched with dirty patches.

Distress encased the disheveled group; there was very little order about their hair or faces. They varied in skin color from creamed-coffee to dark-chocolate to jet-black.

Two men started towards the rear, each carrying large pails. They walked through the foreground as a plume of well-pronounced, white-gray smoke rose in the background. Jason heard another high-pitched scream that was followed by an intriguing burst of a darker, blackish smoke dissecting the billowing gray.

He watched intently after the scream. The emission returned to a whitish gray color but when another woman's voice filled the air, the smoke, very briefly, darkened again before returning to light gray. Distracted by the sight, Jason's ears pulled at his attention as the louder, masculine screams continued in close proximity.

The sequence had been the same: a sudden, loud expression of pain followed by a frantic vibration of chain links, then the connecting chain drawing tight. This sequence repeated itself three times, after which, right on cue, the chain relaxed, losing all tension. Again, three men were led to the center of the courtyard. The third man turned his head back toward the parade formation.

Jason saw a familiar face staring at him. Stunned, he wanted his eyes to blink and, after an excruciatingly long time, they finally did. However, the post-blink image had not altered. There was the face of Kevin Baylor, the old friend with whom he had flown to Okinawa, Japan while in the Marine Corps!

They had not seen each other in 10 years but he was positive that that was Kevin. Jason wondered, "What on earth is Kevin Baylor doing here in chains?"

He tried to call out to him but his vocal chords never responded. Soon Kevin was eliminated from his view, a frustration that caused Jason to actively search for the ability to control his body. His head and eyes were attentive to two men walking back from the rear of the compound.

Returning with buckets filled to the brim with water, they walked over to the far side. Their steps were hurried; water spilled over the edges of the pails. Passing the group in the center of the courtyard, Jason saw that Kevin Baylor had turned and was now facing the same direction as the other men.

A forceful tug at the chain initiated forward movement. And again, his body seemed to understand what his mind did not. He stepped up to the edge of a half wall that opened at an obtuse angle. Jason could now peer in to the corner. There a man stood fanning coals in an aboveground fire pit contained by stones.

Flames roared in plain view, shooting and snapping out a vent near the bottom of the stove. The fire scorched two white-hot metal rods lying within its charred embers. The sight had a dire impact on Jason. The visuals deepened, sound amplified, odors intensified.

Up to this point, by comparison, all smells were faint, all sound mono, and the visuals were that of a 1950's television quality. After looking into the obtuse, Jason was accosted with pungent and palpable emissions, attacking his sense of smell with malevolence.

The accompanying sounds were sharper, with the volume stepped up - from mono to stereo – from stereo to quadraphonic – from quadraphonic to surround. The visuals were similar to sitting through an eye examination in which the optometrist intensifies sight by raising the old blurrier lens and lowering a new, clearer one.

This enhancement allowed for a deeper insight into his situation - from black and white to color - from color to high definition – from high definition to three-dimensional. These senses were heightened in an instant - the instant Jason looked in that corner.

It was there that he witnessed human torture. A man was being positioned to one side of the pit. One of the white-hot rods was lifted from the coals and applied to the man's left shoulder. The metal rods sitting in the furnace were branding irons used on the men in the single file line - the same single file line in which he stood.

The sequence of the chain vibrating-tensing, vibrating-tensing, vibrating-tensing then releasing was such: All the men were tethered together originally; a man was led to the corner and was turned to the right, exposing his left shoulder to the man with the metal rod. Upon touching his flesh with the rod, the branded man shook and convulsed in pain - *the vibration*. The newly branded man was immediately moved to the side and the next man brought to the furnace - *the tension*.

This horror was repeated two more times. Three men branded and connected were then detached from the rest of the group - *the release*. The three were led to the center of the yard.

Jason came to the realization that he was now third in line to be branded and as the next man stepped up the entire scene became even more surreal.

There was a scream. The connecting chain vibrated just as different sounds came from the other side. These recent screams were unlike the previous ones, for these seemed to originate from discomfort rather than pain. Just as the man next to him screamed, water splashed on the far side.

Of more immediate concern was the fact his own chain had tensed; he was ushered into the obtuse.

As the first of his trio turned to face the rear, Jason was struck by the resemblance of this man to his boyhood friend, Allen Cosby. The facial structure was exact. It was uncanny. However, Jason was too concerned with the branding process to concentrate long on what he considered to be a bizarre coincidence. Stepping up two paces, he felt the tautness of the chain links relax just as the second man, the man immediately in front of him, shuffled to the side.

The man's sliced ears were very neat, as if the mutilation had for some reason been done on purpose. Jason noticed the profile of this man as he got in line behind the first - he looked just like Michael Fisher, his old neighborhood buddy. When the man turned, Jason saw it was indeed Michael. He was in the body of a man but still had that same boyish look.

Dazed temporarily, Jason pulled himself back to the moment when the man working the furnace grabbed one of the sizzling irons. His mind wanted to resist, but it was alone, for his body had somehow been conditioned to cooperate. Whoever was in control had been trained to passively accept its fate.

The two men at the branding station forcibly turned Jason's body to the right – there was no physicality felt as they manhandled his shoulders and maneuvered his body. He heard the sizzle of his flesh and smelled the results.

His voice yelled out as his vision violently jerked down and then straight up. Being led away to join the others, his confusion reached an even higher pinnacle. He was branded; he was burnt, yet he felt no pain. Free of discomfort, Jason desperately tried to send a vocal command to his mouth. He tried to call out to Michael Fisher and Allen Cosby. Though he had just heard himself yell out in pain, he made no verbal effort to communicate.

Staggering to the side, he inhaled the burnt-flesh tainted smoke which smoldered from his brand new wound.

Standing alongside Michael and Allen, he too now faced the rear of the courtyard. Through watery vision, he saw that the fence-like wall did indeed extend back behind and connect, but the rear view was quite surprising. There were vintage cannons mounted on platforms, their nozzles protruding over cutout portions of the wall - a canon every 10 feet or so.

Over that wall was a beautiful body of water with white-capped waves starting to peak in the far distance. They casually rode ashore, gently pushed by the sea breeze. The water was a deep, clean-looking, navy blue. Ironically, the hypnotic serenity of surf and sand usually associated with being at the beach was perversely contradicted by the work being performed here.

When his group was brought to the center of the courtyard, his primary view changed to the other side where the women were lined against the far wall. A different group congregated closer, directly across from his new position.

These women were crying. Their contorted faces wet with tears, vertical tracks streaking down their grimy faces. His eyes moved down the line when he saw that one of these women looked like...

Jason's mind reeled - it could not be, but it was - it was Renae Clarke!

There was no question. He wrestled with the idea that Kevin Baylor, Allen Cosby, Michael Fisher, and Renae were all here. Angst combined with disbelief as he wondered, "What the hell is this place?"

Chapter 25

Something was happening. Loud male voices and hysterical female voices combined in frenzied, curious fashion. There were two women, with their backs facing forward, being washed. They were treated roughly while lathered and scrubbed.

Afterward, the men grabbed pails and doused the women with the remaining water. One of the women was lifted off her feet. Her mighty resistance, restricted by the cuffs connecting her hands and her feet, served as little more than a nuisance for the large, burly man handling her.

She was carried to a far corner, deep within the courtyard. Some of the men from both sides walked to that end of the compound.

Their exit opened up Jason' view, allowing the identity of the other woman to be seen. To Jason's absolute amazement, it was Wanda Rodgers. Dripping wet with her arms folded, she stood shivering, nipples erect, silently crying. She didn't have chains or cuffs.

Two men grabbed Wanda and forced her up one of the side staircases, then up the second staircase and through the third level entrance into the building. Soon, after they disappeared inside, another man, better dressed than any of the others working in the courtyard, emerged wearing a long, dark purplish frock jacket. His black boots extended up his leg, forming a cone at the knee.

Stepping down the upper staircase with a gait of supreme confidence, his strides appeared more of a dance than a walk. When he got to the second level landing, he stopped evenly between the two sentries still standing guard at the picketed railing looking out over the courtyard, and began to speak. His stentorian voice brought to a halt all individual activity except for one black man wearing a raggedy shirt and shorts.

No other black person in the courtyard was clothed. More interesting to Jason however, was the fact that this was the only black man not chained.

He ran at a gallop up the right staircase, taking them two at a time, as the well-dressed man continued talking in a language Jason could not begin to understand. Arriving on the landing, he stood off to the side, in a subordinate pose. Head bowed, he maintained sight of the orator with eyeballs looking through the upper echelon of his view.

Seconds later, the fancily clad speaker turned his attention to the black man standing by his side, saying in barely discernible English:

"Boy, since ya'll been free'd up in cha, has ya seen any racism?"

He then turned his gaze to Jason as the awestruck black man, who stood panting at his side, responded imperfectly:

"Well sir, if'n it is, I ain't see's none."

Looking on in stupid bewilderment, Jason was flummoxed. By this point, the men that had taken Wanda into the building were standing outside the opened door. Turning around quickly, the orator hurried up the stairs, and entered the building, stomping the heels of his knee-high boots before closing the large door behind him. Upon his departure, the courtyard became active again, resuming the morose work as agonizing screams and rattling chains combined in aural terror.

A particularly hideous yell caused his body to take notice of the obtuse once again. The first person in line, already branded, was a young slender male. It was Tyrone Polk, the youth choir drummer at church. The usually stoic teenager was shaking and sobbing, a painful expression painted on his face.

His left shoulder had a visible mark resulting from the branding iron. An *M* was burned into the muscle. Red-tinted fleshy matter slowly trickled down his arm.

With the last man branded, their group of three began walking toward Jason in the center of the courtyard. The first person was Tyrone Polk, but just as shocking was the identity of the last man in the group. It was Kenneth Mendes. His light brown skin was noticeable and very much out of place as the rest of the group ranged from dark to extremely dark-complexioned.

That brief, meaningless comparison led Jason to a place of supreme sadness. Who would do this to people in such an organized, methodical way? And what was the ultimate purpose for branding and abusing? Jason was at a low point – sickened by the flesh-burning smell and the torture being performed in this camp.

As quickly as the mental pendulum struck the side of his brain – where he searched for rational reasons why these perversions were occurring, it swung back to the perversions themselves. He was looking across the yard where men, once obstructing the goings-on over on that sideline, had now moved to a far corner. The women on that side were also being branded.

Fiery hot metal applied to their upper buttocks resulted in burnt, fatty flesh darkening the gray smoke of the grill in puffs. Some of the men who had worked the branding operation were now loud and excited as they congregated around that far corner of the compound.

Interspersed between the hoots and howls were muffled sounds of sobbing. A woman sounded as though she were having difficulty breathing. Focusing in that direction, Jason saw the crowd part. The woman had her hands restrained above her head and legs held apart by spikes hammered in the ground through chain links. A man positioned himself in front of her and, as his raggedly-torn pants dropped to the ground, the crowd closed in again.

Then a man walked through the foreground carrying two buckets of water from a cistern in the rear. Jason's head and eyes followed his journey...until he saw the face of another woman.

Violently disturbed, Jason cast his eyes on his wife. The man poured a bucket of water over her head – drenching her from head to foot. He and another began to wash her - scrubbing hard over her breast, mid-section, and pubic area. They turned Callie around to wash her backside.

Horrified, Jason saw her birthmark and tried to scream.

*The El Mina
Courtyard
by Ferris Shelton
1998*

*Steven Quarshie at
El Mina
by Ferris Shelton
1998*

*Cistern In back of
Courtyard
by Ferris Shelton
1998*

*Female Slave Dungeons
by Janice Mazzallo 2018*

Friday

The Knowledge

Chapter 26

Jason's pre-dawn restlessness aroused Callie.

Sitting up in bed, she took the shortest mental route possible from half-sleep to wide awake while studying her husband. Jason slept, laying on his back, sweat rolling down his face the way water would had he just exited a pool.

"Nooooo, Nooooo." That guttural growl was continuous interrupted only by short hiccups with air intake. His arms and legs were so rigidly straight it looked as if his heals might be elevated off the mattress. The tenseness of Jason's body had Callie spellbound – he seemed to be growling out much more air than the hiccups were taking in.

The dim night lamp highlighted Jason's contorted facial features. The space below his eye sockets appeared bruised and his mouth stretched wide, rounded at the corners with only the very center of each lip making contact with the other.

Callie noticed the area within the eye socket. Amazingly, with all the grimacing, Jason's eyeballs were peaceful - gently rolling under smooth eyelids.

Flushed with anxiety, Callie sat riveted by that contrast. Reaching her shaking hands out to Jason and pulling at his arm, she was unable to budge him. His body was flexed mightily; the muscles warm and hard as they looked to be squeezing, with each pulse, the sweat trickling out of his pores. Letting go of his arm, she pulled back and tried to think rationally.

There was a right thing to do now and she desperately considered her options. Time seemed to stand still while Jason's growling grew louder and his sleep more physical. His body started going through the motions of struggle – hands and feet attempting to push away some unseen adversary.

Approaching her wit's end, Callie leaned over and yelled his name, pushing out as hard as she could at his shoulder, resulting in his upper torso going off the mattress. At that exact moment the alarm sounded.

Beeeeeeep, beeeeeeep.

With half his body lurching unsupported off the bed, Jason unexpectedly reached out grabbing Callie' arm. She snatched herself out of his grasp, tumbling to the floor. Standing quickly, Callie walked backwards taking short steps until she could back-up no further.

Her palms turned inwards as her fingers sought to grab a portion of the flat surface. Gracelessly inching towards the door, her hair and pajamas twisted to one side as her body pressed hard against the wall.

Beeeeeeep, beeeeeeep.

...Jason regained real world consciousness as if a light switch had flicked on.

In the blink of an eye, he traversed the boundary between sleep and wakefulness. In an instant his perception went from unsuccessfully trying to scream in the courtyard to being off-balance in his bedroom. When his eyes opened, he felt as though he were not getting enough oxygen and his rapid breathing sought to address that need for more.

The change of scenery was startling, forcing his eyes to adjust from the bright sun of the dream to the wispy early morning light of the bedroom.

Beeeeeeep, beeeeeeep.

Callie was nearly in shock as she had witnessed an incredible transformation. The second Jason's eyes opened, his body sagged; muscles that were tight one second were limp the next. Perspiration, previously oozing out in timed increments - looked to actually recede back into his pores, his skin noticeably clammy.

His eyes however, held the most frightening change of all. Sitting up high, bulging and glassed over when first open, they quickly sank into their sockets - as the whites, seemingly flooded with blood, turned pinkish in color. A darkened, puffy bag drooped under each one.

Beeeeeeep, beeeeeeep.

Callie began to weep, each series of weak sobs hyphenated with hyperventilated breaths.

Being genuinely concerned for Callie, Jason reached out to stop the alarm. Pleading, "Don't cry honey, it's all right," he sprang to his feet. Realizing his weakened physical state immediately, he made a clumsy adjustment to maintain his balance, staggering over to her.

Still clinging to the wall, Callie accelerated her push toward the door. It took an extra step once he finally put his hands on her to gather her completely into his arms.

"I saw you! I saw you while you was sleeping," Callie said unevenly, initially resisting his hold. "You were stiff as a board and sweating...oh my God! I tried to wake you! I tried to move you...but I couldn't and then...Jason, what's happening, baby?"

Her barely coherent words were gargled through a tide of tears. Jason quietly hugged her, allowing her to cry it out. His aching, fatigued body could barely contain her involuntary shaking. When she calmed down, Jason tried to comfort her.

"Callie, it's going to be all right. This dream was more personal. You were in it and..."

"I was in the dream?" asked Callie, beginning to finally relax in his arms.

"Yes, you and Kevin and Michael and Allen and..."

"Who?" Callie inquired, confused by the names.

"And Tyrone and Renae and...and, Wanda Rodgers." A quizzical expression landed on Jason's face as he stated that last name.

"Who's Wanda?" asked Callie, "And who is these other people?"

Jason did not answer her. Instead, with a shift of his head to one side, posture lifting slightly, he whispered slowly, "They were branding people in that courtyard - everybody got branded. And then...oh, shit! Wanda was taken into that building before..."

"Who the hell is Wanda?" Callie demanded.

"The building?" Jason questioned himself. "Wanda was brought into the building before the man spoke." Darting his eyes from one side to the other as if optically seeking elusive answers to unstated, internal questions he said, "Maybe I can find it."

Charging out of the bedroom, mustering energy from a source other than physical, he scooted down the hall, past the spare bedroom with Callie on his heels, firing question after question. Without responding, Jason continued to the office, sat down at the desk and turned on the computer.

"Jason! Don't you hear me talkin' to you?" demanded Callie impatiently.

"Callie, I have something to do right now - so, please honey, this is not your time."

"My time!" She was nearly yelling. "I'm not some of the time. I'm all of the time!"

"Come on now, Callie, I don't mean it like that. Aren't you hungry? I'm starving," Jason replied, not wanting to get anything started. "Why don't you fix some breakfast and let me do this?"

"Do what?"

"Think about the dream while it's still fresh in my mind, honey."

"I don't know - maybe I'll make us breakfast," responded Callie. After hesitating briefly she added, "Maybe - after you answer one question."

"Okay Sweetie," Jason said as he took his hand off the computer mouse while the machine went through the start-up diagnostic checks, "One question."

"Who are these people you are dreaming about and what are you looking for?"

"Sweetheart, you know the people; remember Kevin Baylor, my old Marine Corps buddy and Michael Fisher and Allen Cosby from Chicago and Wanda Rodgers, the woman candidate for the AP position at Edwards."

Jason paused, looking to see the computer had finished booting up before clicking the Internet icon and adding, "I don't know exactly what I'm looking for, but I think somewhere on the Internet there may be an answer. Now, I'm really hungry. You know I haven't been eating well. So, could you please make breakfast?"

He typed in his password and pressed 'enter.' While it connected Callie said, "Well, why are you dreaming about Wanda - what's her name?"

"You see Callie, there's never really one question."

With tears rising along her lids and eventually squeezed out at the corners of each eye, Callie's voice elevated in volume and pitch, "Jason, I asked you yesterday to stop keeping secrets from me and you promised! You been having these dreams and I didn't even know how serious they was until..." Her statement trailed off, dripping with emotion.

"Now honey, don't cry. Please don't cry. Callie how can I tell you something I don't know? That's what I'm trying to do - to find out what's going on. I'm just saying the answer may be on the Internet someplace and I'm not finding it because you keep asking me questions that I have not found answers to yet. So please, why don't you leave me alone for a while so I can see if there are any clues on the Net? I will explain everything to you later, I promise."

With a cajoling squeeze of her hand he added, "I'm honestly hungry. I'll answer all your questions today. I promise you - today you will know all that I know."

They stood there in awkward silence until he mouthed the word "please" and glanced towards the office door. Callie made a sound through clenched teeth and closed lips. It was a sound he'd heard many times before but had never quite figured out how to replicate.

She spun and headed for the door. Jason sat down and clicked for a search engine, fully aware that she had stopped, turned, and stood in the doorway. After the search engine loaded, Jason typed in "Africa" and hit 'enter,' never looking up at her.

After a few seconds, Callie left the room.

Chapter 27

The search engine returned over 500,000 sites containing the word "Africa" prominently. Jason scrolled through screen after screen not sure of what he was looking for. A few pages in was the official governmental website of South Africa and he clicked the "More Like This" button before going into the site itself. He spent time reading through South African websites focusing on culture, customs, and people - then he went to sites of other countries he knew of in Africa – Ethiopia, Eritrea, Kenya, and Somalia.

Their official governmental sites were interesting but nothing in any of them seemed relevant, so after nearly an hour of searching, he stood from the chair and paced the room, considering the prospect of going through website after website without purposefully looking for anything specific. He wondered how to limit the group.

Callie returned to the room carrying a tray with breakfast for two. Bracing it on her thigh and against the corner of the desk, she started shifting away some of the clutter.

"Have you found anything yet?"

"No, I haven't, but I really just started. Not knowing any of the specifics is like looking for a needle in a haystack," stated Jason dejectedly. He removed a couple of paper stacks and pushed the monitor to the side while asking, "Hey, what was that word Kenny used yesterday when he mentioned the castles on the coast of Africa?"

"Wasn't it *latitude?*" answered Callie.

"Yeah, I think that was it," Jason stated appreciably. "Maybe I'll narrow my search to a specific area of Africa. I can probably find a map somewhere."

"Well Jason, Encarta will have a fairly current map of Africa."

"Hmmm, that would be faster," agreed Jason, putting the Encarta CD in the drive.

"If you don't know what you're looking for, how will you know when you find it?" asked Callie casually.

"More questions, Callie," responded Jason as the voice of Nelson Mandela signaled that Encarta had loaded.

"Don't start with me, Jason!" She snapped. "I made your breakfast; the least you can do is let me help you look. Come on and eat before the food gets cold."

"Let me print out a map of Africa and then I'll sit and eat with you if you promise to leave me to go through the Internet sites alone. I'm not being mean honey; it's just that it's a one-person job."

"All right Jason, dag. I gotta get ready for work anyway," said an annoyed Callie. "Are you going to work today or what?"

"I don't know yet. You know, Africa is so large; to get the entire continent Encarta forces you to print three maps." He processed the three print requests and wheeled his chair closer to Callie while the printer began printing.

"Thank you, sweetie, for making breakfast. I'm starving,"

"You're welcome. So, what do you think you're looking for?"

"Well honey, I think the building is the key. In the dream Tuesday night I walked to a white building that stood tall when compared to everything else around. Wednesday night, I was in a dark room with only one window high on a wall. There was no way of knowing for sure if that room was in the building, but last night's dream was at the same building as Tuesday night's. I'm sure of it."

"Kenny talked about slave castles yesterday. Do you think the building in the dreams is a slave castle?"

"I don't know, Callie. But I'm going to search everything connected to buildings or castles in Africa."

"You said I was in the dream?"

"Yes, this is the first dream where I saw recognizable faces. People from my past and people I know presently were in the same predicament I was..."

"I was chained in the dream?"

"Yes, Callie."

"Was I branded, too?" Callie inquired excitably.

"I couldn't tell if you were..."

"So, what was I doing?"

"Okay Callie, here we go. Before I can answer one question, you're throwing another one at me. Right now, I have to find information on the building."

"Okay-okay, Jason, just one more question."

"There's never just one more question."

"Don't be like that. If you finished eating, I'll leave after one last question."

"All right Callie, I'm done. What is this one last question?"

"Why were you screaming 'no, no' in your sleep? What were you seeing in the dream?"

Jason did not want to tell her that in the dream men were preparing her to be raped. The very thought of those last few moments of the dream turned Jason's stomach.

"Callie, you know I love you with all my heart," Jason stated in a quiet but serious voice. "What I saw was very unpleasant, but that can't be my focus right now. I will give you all the details of the dream later. I promise, okay?"

"This unpleasant thing," Callie paused and stared into Jason's eyes in a way that made him uncomfortable, "Did it have anything to do with me?"

Jason turned away, rolling his chair back to the computer monitor and pulled the three printouts from the printer. While studying the output he casually stated, "What did I tell you? There's never really one last question."

Callie stood, stacked the plates on the tray and while walking out muttered, "This may be the last meal I prepare for you if you don't start treating me better." She left the room in an exaggerated huff. Jason looked up and smiled. He loved her – attitude and all.

Of the three segmented maps of Africa - western, eastern and southern - the western map had a long coastline stretching from east to west. Focusing on the countries along this coast, Jason realized he had never heard of most of them. The one country he recognized nearest to this area was Nigeria, though he was not sure how or why he had ever heard of that one.

The other countries were Liberia, Cote D' Ivoire, Ghana, Togo, Benin, and Cameroon. Jason went to their official government websites and read through each, spending over an hour. He never knew that in the 19th century the United States government agreed to resettle captured slaves in Liberia. The Cote D' Ivoire official website was in French, and he was unable to understand it, but other sites told of a country previously named Ivory Coast.

Ghana was an impressive country with one of the strongest economies in all of Africa and was the first to gain independence from colonial European powers. Togo was first a colony of Germany. Jason had not remembered Germany being involved in colonizing Africa.

There was a website about Benin, formerly known as Dahomey, that sorrowfully apologized for the role it played in facilitating the sale of African prisoners in the slave trade. He learned that Nigeria, an oil-rich nation and a member of OPEC, has the largest population of any country in Africa.

Though the information was interesting, there was no mention of castles or even architecture in any of the websites. Jason stood up and stretched his arms. He was getting tired and frustrated. As he paced the room, he considered giving up, thinking there may not be a real-world connection to these crazy dreams after all.

Jason thought back to what Dr. Caswell said about it being up to him to find the answer and how his body and mind would not hold up indefinitely were the dreams to continue over an extended period.

There had to be a hint about this building someplace on the Internet. He sat back down in front of the computer and mumbled to himself, "I've got to work while it's daylight because when the night comes..."

Allowing the open-ended part of that thought to linger for just a moment - for he dared not dwell on it too long, Jason shuddered at the thought of another dream. He feared what he already knew just as much as the unknown terrors lurking in future night's sleep. However, "Zero Hour" occurred when he closed his eyes at the end of the day.

Night and unavoidable sleep would come soon enough. There was time to learn something about what was happening, feeling acute desperation, he performed a search on the word 'castle.'

The results were not encouraging. Scrolling through the pages he discovered that most were centered on castles in Europe. Of one thing he was sure – if he was at a castle, it was not in Europe. He did another search on slaves with equally disappointing results. Most dealt with American slavery, with nary a mention of castles.

Jason spent the better part of another hour fruitlessly scrolling through castle and slave websites as his eyes tired from looking at the computer monitor and his patience dwindled. When he searched on "slave castle" all the sites were pornographic.

After paging through a number of search screens, he felt he was getting farther away from where he needed to be.

Standing, he paced the floor again, sensing something of use was out there someplace. "But how in the world do I find it?" he wondered.

Chapter 28

Needing a break, Jason went downstairs for a cup of coffee. Before turning for the kitchen, he saw Callie sitting in the den, fingering through her Grandmother's antique Bible. She had taken it down from the mantel and sat on the couch, carefully going through the fragile pages.

He asked her what she was doing to which she smartly replied, "I know you ain't asking me no questions!"

Callie looked up and smiled, "I called Edwards and talked to Terri. I told her you wouldn't be in today and I called the Community Center also and told them I'd be in around 12."

Jason thanked her, got his coffee and went back upstairs to the office. Sitting at the computer he searched "Africa" again, clicking "next 10" many, many times, only casually noticing the summaries as they went by. He had already gone through 20 or 30 pages the first time through. As he clicked away, a link called "Historic Africa" appeared.

Jason had the clicking routine so well timed he went by the page that contained the link before he realized completely what it was. He scrolled to the top of the screen to go back and clicked "more like these" at Historic Africa.

Scrolling through the results, he saw a link to the "History of the slave trade in Ghana." He clicked to go there. The first available site was "Cape Coast Slave Castle." Jason entered the website. A picture of a large white building appeared with text underneath. He stared at the building and although there were some similar features, it was not the building in the dreams. Reading the text, he was surprised the building had been on UNESCO's World Heritage List of protected sites since 1979.

There was also mention of a dungeon that housed the captured Africans until the ships used to transport them to the New World arrived. He exited that site. The next was called *El Mina*. Jason thought back to the dream last night, recalling how the branding iron left an *"M"* burned into the flesh of Tyrone Polk.

His heart began to race and in the back of his mind he heard the faint beat of a drum. With more than a little apprehension, Jason clicked onto the *El Mina* site. Slowly the picture came into view and as the photograph of *El Mina* cleared, Jason sat wide-eyed. He recognized the dormers and cannons. He recognized the shape of the building with the exterior wall higher on the ocean side. He recognized the stairs and arches. The building in his dreams was real – it was *El Mina*.

This stunning revelation was cathartic.

Staring at the computer monitor, Jason felt a freedom beginning to enfold. It was as if a large, chilled drop of molasses-thick oil had been released atop his head. As this sensation slowly – ever so slowly – moved stealthily down his tired and fatigued body, he felt a spiritual elation that brought tears to his eyes and a vague joy to his heart.

He felt rejuvenated and renewed. It was a refreshing touch – an ecstasy - affecting body, mind, and soul.

Ring - Ring.

The phone rang as he read the accompanying text on the *El Mina* website.

Ring – Ring.

"Jason, you gonna answer the phone?" called Callie from downstairs.

He clicked the print icon and picked up the phone.

"Hello."

"Hi Jason, guess what?" It was Kenny Mendes. "I think I found the language you are speaking in the vision."

Jason glanced at the printer as the picture of *El Mina* was being layered across the paper.

"Uh...what?" Jason said half listening.

"You're speaking an African dialect," a fast-talking Mendes went on. "I think it's called Twi. It's an African language native to the Ashanti people. Jason...Jason, are you listening?"

"Yeah, yeah I'm listening," responded a now more interested Jason.

"The word Callie heard you chanting Wednesday, well I played that portion of the tape for a few people and a Dr. Stephen Quarshie says it sounds like his language."

"What language does he speak?" asked Jason.

"It's called Twi."

"Tree?"

"No, there's a 'w' not an 'r'," Mendes corrected. "The words you used, *'kwan no fefini'* – means 'half' or 'halfway' in Twi."

"This Dr. Stephen Quarshie, is he from Ghana?" inquired Jason.

"Yes...yes, he is. He is Ashanti and the Ashanti people are primarily located in Ghana," stated a surprised Mendes. "How could you have known that?"

"I've been on the Internet all morning and I found this place off the coast of..."

"Jason, Jason!" Callie was screaming at the top of her lungs, running up the stairs.

Jason covered the receiver with his hand and called out, "What is it Callie? What's wrong?"

"Look Jason!" Callie had the antique Bible cupped in her arms with the fingers of her right hand tucked in at the closed end of the open book. She sat the Bible down right on the keyboard causing the computer to beep.

"Callie, be careful," Jason said, taking the Bible and placing it in his lap. Putting the phone back up to his ear, he said, "Hold on, Kenny."

"Is that Kenny?" asked an excited Callie. She reached over with her left hand and pressed on the speakerphone. "Hi Kenny, I found the language. It's Hebrew."

"Hebrew!" Laughed Mendes. *"It's not Hebrew, Callie it's..."*

"Jason, look at this," Callie stated loudly, cutting Mendes off in mid-sentence. She gently rolled the pages back to where the fingers of her right hand were inserted. While doing this, she kept the fingers of her left hand tucked into the Bible where it had once been opened.

She took her right index finger and pointed – from an up-side-down vantage point – to Isaiah and said, "You see, Jason?"

"I see Isaiah," said Jason. "What's that got to do with any...?"

"Next to Isaiah, Jason," Callie was very nearly shouting. "See - the Hebrew translation."

Jason looked over to a word he could not pronounce. He spoke phonetically, *"Ye Shay Ahu.* Hey, that's the..."

"That's right. Now look." With her left hand she folded back the same pages that had just been moved. "You said there was a "30" and a "26" under the message, or over it, whatever. But, read Isaiah 30:26."

Jason read the verse and the hairs on his arm raised as his blood chilled. It was the message he had seen Wednesday:

ISAIAH

30:26

"Moreover, the Light of the Moon will be
as the Light of the Sun
and the Light of the Sun will be Sevenfold,
As the Light of Seven Days
In the Day that the Lord Bindeth up the Breach of His People
and Healeth the Stroke of their Wounds."

"What's going on, Jason?" asked Mendes over the speakerphone.

Jason explained to Mendes what just happened while reaching for the completed printout of the *El Mina* slave castle and handing it to Callie, gesturing for her to read. He waited until she finished the text, expecting a barrage of questions, but she just looked up from the paper with wondering eyes.

Jason asked Mendes to catch Callie up on what he found as he sat and pondered this rush of information.

"This is pretty deep," said Mendes, after getting Callie to come close to properly pronouncing Twi and after she read aloud the Bible verse. *"One could interpret the seven days of the Bible reference to mean one maybe two more dreams, Jason."*

"That's how I figure it, too," agreed Jason. "Especially when the tree word...I mean the Twi word is factored into the equation. The vision occurred Wednesday, three dreams in and two dreams ago. Kenny, I've been on the Internet all morning and I came across a website on the *El Mina* Slave Castle. That's the building in the dreams."

"Ah, El Mina,*"* commented Mendes. *"That was one of the worst ones. It had a terrible reputation and was one of the larger, most active of the slave castles. But as I recall, they all had what was known as a 'door of no return.'"*

"The printout mentioned something about that," Callie interjected. "What is it?"

"The slave traders needed to discourage any inclination the captives may have had for an uprising so the slave castles provided very little food to the captured Africans," Mendes said solemnly. *"This was done not only to weaken them - the men especially - but also to emaciate them, to make them smaller. When it came time to exit the slave castle for the ships, the Africans had to fit through a small opening called the 'door of no return.' The stories told back in Africa are that if an African was too big to get through this space, he was killed at the castle.*

Either way, once captured or sold to a slave castle, Africans were shipped off to North America or the Caribbean, or they were killed. Never were they freed to continue life as they knew it in Africa."

"That's pretty interesting, Kenny. But what does it have to do with the dreams?" asked Jason.

"Well, if somehow one were to experience an African's journey into slavery then there are several critical points along the way. Some are well known and obvious. Others have been lost or deemed not important enough to be included in the recording of slavery's history," Mendes' words had a strange stilted cadence. *"Being captured or sold into slavery and surviving the Trans-Atlantic voyage are commonly known, but one of the first tests of survival was the little-known fact of having to fit through this small opening exiting one of these castles. Jason, it was do or die, sudden death with no third option."*

"And you think Jason will have to get through this 'door of no return' in the next dream?" inquired Callie.

"The Bible verse suggests it may not be the next dream but the last," Mendes theorized. *"And yes, I think Jason will have to get through the 'door of no return.' The experience would not be complete without it."*

"Hmmm, I see," said Jason.

"But, don't worry, Jason. Remember what Dr. Caswell said, this was brought on because you somehow got out of balance – lost your equilibrium. You are doing exactly the right thing by attempting to learn as much as possible about this situation," said a more upbeat Mendes. *"How do you feel anyway? I'm guessing you had a dream last night."*

"Yeah, but I'll have to tell you about it later. I feel a lot better though, Kenny. Seeing that building – *El Mina* was, was..." Jason was lost for words.

"I can imagine. Listen Jason, keep doing your research, I believe the more you learn the better. Knowledge is power my

friend," said Mendes, beginning to sound hurried. *"Callie, are you still there?"*

"Yes I am," responded Callie.

"Finding that Bible verse was brilliant," commented Mendes. *"We are armed with a lot more information now than we had yesterday. But the Hebrew translation ties it together and suggests there is an end to these dreams and that they won't go on indefinitely."*

"Thank you, Kenny," Callie said while reaching to pinch Jason in his side.

"With that I'll say bye, but I'll call you later on."

"All right Kenny. Thanks man."

"Bye Kenny."

Jason sat up to disengage the speakerphone. He carefully closed the Bible and set it aside. Leaning back in the chair, he contemplated his unplanned journey. Why was this happening to him? How could this be happening? Those questions were open-ended with potential answers - or theories - not readily available. But something else - a correctable left uncorrected - lingered as if an important piece was still not in place. It called on him even as he struggled to discern its exact nature.

"Are you okay, honey?" asked Callie noticing his strange look.

"Yeah, I'm just thinking," Jason replied distantly. "You know, I think I'm going in to work. I can print all the information I can find on *El Mina* faster there."

Chapter 29

Jason drove into midtown Atlanta in the early afternoon, arriving to work at 1:30 P.M. Since he had seen that castle on the Internet, he felt more like his old self, a little tired but with renewed spirit. As he walked into the lobby of the administrative area, he saw Renae at the receptionist desk.

"Hey, what are you doing here? I heard you were going to be out today."

"I started feeling better later in the morning," he said as he motored through. Walking past the desk he remembered their conversation earlier and stopped. "You know, you asked my advice on something and I said I would get back to you. I've thought about it and I suggest you don't do anything you don't want to do. And should you choose not, you won't have to worry about getting fired. Not for that."

"Don't worry, Mr. Scott. I'm not even really thinking about seeing him socially, but it's good to hear you say that."

"Just handle the work-related business and everything will be fine."

He entered his office; sat at his desk and clicked to the Internet, hoping his company's Cyber Patrol would not restrict him from accessing the slave castle and Ghanaian websites. He was able to query and view the sites and spent an hour queuing print jobs for later. Eventually, Bob Farrington walked in to his office.

"How ya doin, bud?" greeted a cheerful Farrington. "I heard you had a touch of the flu."

"I'm fine Bob. It was just a 24-hour thing," Jason said not looking up from his computer monitor, before adding, "But, I'm busy; what can I do for you?"

"Well, I wasn't sure if you'd heard, but Diane Scosia turned down the AP super position, something about the commute being too far."

"Really!" replied a shocked Jason looking up from the computer screen.

"Yeah, I guess Clay has decided to begin the search again next week."

"Begin the search?...excuse me, Bob." Maddeningly annoyed, Jason rose from his desk and walked out of the office, leaving Bob Farrington standing there.

He walked down the hall to Terri McGowan's office where he found her and Clay Calhoun in conference. He leaned his head in and said, "Good afternoon."

Surprised, Terri McGowan said, "Oh! Hi Jason, I didn't know you were in today. How do you feel?"

"I've felt better," replied Jason, accepting the inquiry on his health as an invitation to enter the office.

"Do you have the flu?" asked McGowan.

"No, it's just a cold," stated Jason, leaning back against the office wall. "I heard Diane Scosia turned down the accounts payable position and that we are going to restart the search."

"We're going to get one or two more candidates to provide us with a choice," interjected Calhoun.

"Why?" responded Jason, never taking his eye from Terri McGowan. "We've gone through that process already and filtered it down to two. If the first choice didn't accept the job, why aren't we offering it to the second choice? Terri, I don't want to go another two or three weeks processing AP invoices."

"I can understand that Jason," said McGowan.

"All right, Jason. We'll fast track the hiring for that position," offered Calhoun. He then turned his attention to papers on the desk; the implication being that the conversation was over.

Jason put his head down; he was very frustrated. He needed that AP position filled first and foremost, but what really stuck in his craw was the unfairness of the decision. Without raising his head and without forethought Jason blurted, "Are we equal opportunity employers or just equal opportunity interviewers."

"Jason if you don't think there is a language problem, then I agree we should give Wanda Rodgers a shot," Terri McGowan asserted quickly.

"Terri, she speaks English with an accent no more difficult to understand than someone from Boston or West Virginia."

"Are you sure you can make this work, Jason?" asked a still reluctant sounding Calhoun.

"Yes Clay, I'm confident Wanda Rodgers can do the job," replied Jason.

Clay Calhoun agreed to give Wanda Rodgers the chance. Terri McGowan said she would ask Human Resources to offer the position to Ms. Rodgers that day. Jason went back to his now empty office and continued to queue website printouts. Just prior to five o'clock, he got an e-mail from Terri McGowan:

> *Hi Jason,*
> *I was going to talk to you about Wanda Rodgers*
> *and form a united front for when we all discussed it.*
> *Your way was just as effective, if less diplomatic.*
> *Good job.*
> *Terri McGowan*
> P.S. Wanda accepted the position. TM

Being Friday, the office cleared out early. At 5:30 Jason released the print jobs he had stored in the queue all afternoon. He stayed and read through the printouts until past seven o'clock when the phone rang. It was Callie.

"If you think you're going to get out of telling me about that dream because you're staying at work all night, you're wrong. I'm going to wait up."

"Hi Callie, I'm just reading through some things," replied Jason. "I'll be leaving here soon."

"Make it very soon. I'm ordering a pizza and I need you to pick it up."

"All right honey, I'm leaving now."

Jason drove home reviewing all the things he learned that day on slave castles and the kind of places they must have been. The dreams, as terrible an experience as they were, could not come close to duplicating the horrors of living in a castle 24/7 for up to six to eight weeks.

That dungeon would have been the place of confinement for some or all that time. Deep emotion set in at the very thought of enduring a place like *El Mina* for a week or longer. It would be a test of anyone's determination to survive through the very worst of times.

Once there, a man or woman could not hope to escape, while the horrors inside must have incited all to seek a way. A way back to whatever, however things were before - before that dungeon. Tears streamed down his face as he drove home with no effort made to hold them back.

The dungeon, the courtyard, the entire slave castle experience was a real part of so many peoples' lives. Jason had a unique empathy that brought to his heart a true sorrow and newfound respect for his ancestors.

Wrestling with his emotions all the way, Jason went home, ate pizza with Callie and shared with her the latest dream. But he did not mention the rape. When asked what caused the shouting that morning, he said she was about to get branded. They watched a movie and were very affectionate with each other, not often out of physical contact for the entire evening.

Jason felt real closeness to her – that oneness that made their relationship so special. After the movie, they went upstairs to bed. Once Callie fell asleep Jason lay in bed reading more of the output on the slave castles. Initially her rest stayed near the surface because his every movement caused her to groggily turn around to look for him. Eventually, sleep deepened and she quit reacting.

Around 10:30 Kenny Mendes called. Speaking in low tone, Jason told him about the dream last night.

"Wow, that's a wild story!" stated Mendes. After inquiring about a few more details of the dream, Mendes finally asked the most pressing of questions, "Jason, are you afraid of going to sleep tonight?"

"No Kenny, I'm really not. I was earlier today, but not anymore. In a way, I'm looking forward to the dream tonight and hopefully the end of this entire thing."

It was 11 p.m. when they finally said goodnight. Jason reached into his nightstand drawer, picking up his seldom read New International Version of the Bible. He read Isaiah 30:26 a couple of times.

Feeling he had done all he could that day, Jason lay in bed with eyes open, trying to measure his feelings. He felt good, somewhat apprehensive but with a little more confidence.

Turning out the light, he took a deep breath, closed his eyes, and in a short time was fast asleep.

Friday Night

The Departure

Chapter 30

A whistling wind accompanied rain.

Both tranquil and disturbing, the sounds were distant, neither affecting his immediate area, which was dry and calm. It was dark yet somehow shadows were created in fits and spurts.

Jason heard two distinct sounds associated with the rain; one crisp and constant - trees, the roof, the ground and other things out in the elements being pummeled by the raindrops; and another less familiar. It was chaotic, sounding as though the natural flow of water was interrupted, gathered, and then released. It decorated the monotonous rhythm of the rain as vigorously as string instruments playing expressive allegro.

He smelled musty human odor in his midst; then heard voices whispering in close proximity. Together they triggered an invading claustrophobic feeling. He could scarcely see anything, yet he felt crowded. Although his breathing was normal, he found himself impatiently waiting for each breath and desperately wanting to take in more air than his body was drawing.

The tight confines had a stranglehold on his consciousness, so he sent out a critically important command to make an adjustment - to find a less crowded place. That expeditious instruction went out with rising import, for he was surrounded by a ghastly, suffocating aura.

The completeness by which his body ignored this urgent command caused his discomfort level to soar.

An excruciatingly long period of time elapsed before a creaking sound refocused his attention. He listened resolutely in hopes of hearing another clue. Eventually believing the noise stemmed not so much from the front as up top; his immediate area was calm but someone was walking above his head.

A twinkle of light flashed through the compartment. It was a blur, ending almost as abruptly as it began. Seconds later another sliver darted through and it, too, vanished quickly. Jason was sure whatever hindered the light did so from the bottom up.

Startled by the light the first time, he was more prepared for the second burst, and used the opportunity to glimpse and mentally record his surroundings. That claustrophobic feeling, in the initial stages of leveling off, surged again as what he saw looped through his mind.

He was in a small, tight area and it was overcrowded with people. Not everyone was at the same level as the backs and shoulders of the people directly in front of him were elevated, with the people in front of them elevated even further.

The light, just like the sound earlier, originated not so much from the front, but more specifically from up above.

There was also action associated with the light's second appearance, as people directly in front of him began to stir. Jason sensed movement and a slight updraft of the surrounding air. Soon his head looked down, without mental stimulus, to a space cleared in front of him. The space was a step roughly eight inches above where he was currently standing.

A man to the right stepped up onto the barely visible space followed by the man next to him. Jason saw his manacled and cuffed foot rise. An X-shaped chain connected the cuffs on his ankles with those on his wrists. He planted a foot on the step and his vision slowly rose.

Jason's step-up dramatically changed his position. The higher vantage point was better lit for he had moved from being below floor level – actually under the floor with his view blocked by floor boards – to being at floor level. He now had limited visibility of the more open expanse above and the tight confines below.

The sight of those open spaces was enough to soothe that dominating feeling of being closed-in.

This current position also revealed a tall ceiling above, reflecting oversized human shadows busily moving about. He was standing three abreast in a steep stairwell. His position was nearest the wall on his left side, which continued from the dark area beneath the floor to the rather large room above. A hinged door swung up into the open area and leaned against this wall.

Occasionally voices spoke a language other than that being whispered. There was also a strong current of air intermittently blowing down the stairwell, carrying with it the cool, damp, refreshing breeze of rain, coupled with a strong briny scent. Having his eyes, ears, and nose at floor level forced him to gather his intelligence from above.

His direct view was of dark, sweaty, bare backs. The three men in front began, one-by-one, to move up and forward, making another step available for his flank. He now knew the drill and impatiently waited for the two men in his rank to make their step upward.

Before the first man moved, his vision began to change. It was as though the natural blinking motion were reversed; his eyes seemed to stay closed for many seconds and then open for a millisecond only to close again for a much longer duration.

Eventually, an image flickered before finally occupying Jason's entire span of view. He was not sure, but he thought his eyes might be closed. His reasoning was based on a new, mysterious image – which had become prominent, replacing the view of sweaty backs.

There was a child, a small boy of maybe six or seven, laughing and running in an open field. This sunny day found other children chasing him around in a frolicking manner resembling play.

Suddenly, as if someone lifted a shade, the sweaty backs reappeared. After waiting for the other two men in his row to step up, his body gingerly did the same. Jason was deliriously confounded when right after that step, the child returned to his view. He was now sure that his eyes were indeed closed.

Smiling broadly and appearing winded, the child ran with only a piece of cloth tied around his narrow hips and beads around his waist and neck. Glancing backward and cutting sharply to avoid the other children gaining at him, the child eventually fell to the ground in a field of short, soft grass. There the other children, all of whom were laughing and giggling in delight, pounced upon him. Seconds later, something attracted their attention as all stood, looking around.

The young child ran toward an adult figure standing in a path. Jason saw that it was that of a woman. She was standing erect, with a flat tray holding some kind of fruit perfectly balanced on top of her head. Her garment was long, down to her ankles, and appeared to wrap around her body, and tuck in above her breast.

As the boy approached, the woman reached up with both hands and removed the platform of fruit. There was a cloth wound tightly around the crown of her head. It was flattened and her natural bouffant raised the cloth two or three inches, giving it the look of a close-hovering halo.

The boy leapt into the woman's arms. After the embrace, the woman reached down and grabbed a piece of fruit. She handed the boy the treat and placed the platform back atop her head before clutching the child's hand and leading him down the path. The woman walked with perfect posture as the child skipped and jumped at her side eating the fruit.

The image faded and Jason realized his eyes opened.

His body had already moved up one more step but almost immediately after opening his eyes another stair cleared. Upon stepping up he saw the room much better. There was a large, heaping pile in a far corner. Wide at the base and irregularly mounded topside, it stood out as there were no furnishings any-where in the room. With only dim light available, this pile off in the shadows looked odd and formless.

It sat in a far corner and Jason saw that the walls of the upper expanse angled oddly, slanting more than 90-degrees. The room appeared to have a hexagon shape.

Suddenly, as if a flashlight were turned on, a sulfurous yellow beam of light cut across the room. It carved through the dark-ness like a laser. Its height no more than 12 to 15 inches - and narrowing in its descent as it shone through the room.

The brightness bent downward, casting better contoured shadows of people against the walls. The light also served to illume actual people. A man flashed into view on the right side. Walking through the light quickly, he was visible only a second. Others followed.

Jason stared at the men walking in and out of the light. They would, like magic, appear then disappear. Only their mid-torsos were visible, for the light did not shine high enough for faces to be revealed. The now you see them, now you don't act was mes-merizing as they flashed through - sometimes forward, some-times backward, never lingering long in view.

Chapter 31

Rapid blinking again, as his eyes involuntarily closed. Another image behind his eyelids came into focus. Immediately trying to concentrate only on his hearing, he heard the rain and wind, the sounds so prevalent earlier, fade away, leaving only silence.

A teenager and an adult man walked through a densely vegetated area. Both carried sharpened wooden staffs. They stopped as the man instructed the teenager by pointing to something on the ground. The youngster nodded in a manner that indicated comprehension and respect for the elder. Then the man walked to a nearby tree and climbed it. His legs and arms were powerful.

Quickly scampering to a low, sturdy branch, he then beckoned for the youth. The teenager struggled, but managed to join the man in short order.

They sat on the tree limb with staffs, looking like weapons, at the ready. The elder and the teenager appeared to be very close as the man looked at the youngster with obvious pride, all the while admonishing him to be quieter. He pointed down to the ground at what looked to be an approaching boar. The teenager stealthily coiled his arm and hurled the spear.

It lodged in the neck of the beast who, after running but a few feet, slumped down to the ground. The man enthusiastically congratulated the boy, even as the wide-eyed teenager - impervious to the man's excitement, stared down at the gasping animal. After climbing down from the tree, they walked over to the creature. The adult smiled broadly as the teenager timidly approached the animal he had just killed.

The image faded and his eyes reopened. Dizzy and frustrated, Jason was unable to concentrate on his surroundings, though he desperately wanted to. Stepping up another stair, he was now standing on the floor of the room - up and out of the stairwell. The beam of light streaking through the room was coming in from a window-size egress about two feet up from the floor.

A vertical rectangle about three feet tall by one foot wide, it was the only opening in the area, other than the hatchway he had just climbed through.

That window was not in his straight-on view, for the wall that contained the opening was at an angle. Still, he saw it was raining very hard outside. At intervals the wind would drive the rain through the pane-less opening, wetting the ledge and floor directly beneath.

Three men walked briskly through the light. They were seen out of the corner of his vision, as his head had not acknowledged their movement.

Each man passing in and out of the beam earlier was topless and dirty with olive skin much darkened by the sun. However, the latest three were black. Confusion reigned as Jason wondered what was going on, when – to his absolute annoyance – his eyes closed once more.

This time an untenable sadness swayed through his brain as an image started.

A young man stood nervously in front of three people – a middle-age man and woman, and a damsel. Sitting on a felled tree trunk, the older couple looked up at the younger man disapprovingly. The young lady sat with her legs facing away from the three of them, trying unsuccessfully not to sneak a peek over her shoulder at the young man.

She was dark and lovely, wearing a colorful headband matching the wrap around her body. Reaching to his side, the young man pulled out a small leather sack and handed it to the older man after displaying its contents in his hand. The bag was full of gold nuggets and other shiny items. The older man's look did not change.

The young man then offered the elder an animal pelt of a female lion. It was tan-brown with dark patches at the end of the arms and legs. The neck portion was intact and was without the hairy mane. This gift apparently pleased the senior man, as he wrapped it around his shoulders, accepting it with a nod of approval.

But, after briefly consulting with the matriarch, a stern look returned to the eldest man's face. Retreating backwards the young man returned with neatly folded red and black cloth. Offering it to the woman, the item was accepted and she whispered to the elder man. Together they stood and hugged the young woman with warm, loving embraces, motioning her hand to the young man.

The two knew they would now 'jump the broom' and they walked away, heads bowed smiling sheepishly at each other. The young man had paid the dowry for his new bride.

Gradually, Jason recovered his eyesight. Although the image had receded, the view of the room looked as though it was being seen through a window being rinsed with water. Having been deeply moved by the images, Jason came to realize he had been observing someone's heartfelt, personal musings.

The subtle implication of loss and the yearning for what once was had him wondering whose memories they were. The boy, the teenager and the young man had all looked to be the same person. "But who?" he thought.

When his vision cleared completely, Jason saw a man stepping into the light. He did not dart through like the other men had, but instead entered the light in the middle of the room and stayed within its illumination, shuffling toward the wet, reflecting opening. The light beam brightened his stomach and upper thighs, highlighting a thin, tightly-wrapped piece of cloth around his waist. He put both arms up, grabbing the high ledge.

Leaning over, he put his head and shoulders through the opening, attempting to slither his way out.

He made an awkward exit. His legs sprang up just as he slid his stomach through, but they caught on the top of the opening. Fortunately for him, though kicking wildly, he was eased down through the opening. With that window cleared again, Jason saw a heavy piece of chain, extending from outside toward the interior of the room. The links were as thick as a man's fist.

Another man – this time quite a bit smaller – stepped into the light and started for the egress. Upon arrival, he easily fit through, jumping from the ledge with grace. He compensated for the heavy chain restricting his free movement by swinging his body out first, then releasing his hold on the upper ledge.

The chain lying at the base of the window lifted when the man stepped on the ledge. After he jumped out, metal rubbing against metal was heard and the thick chain settled back on the ledge with a thud.

A third man entered the light, meandering his way to the opening. He was quite a bit larger than the two preceding men. Lifting one leg onto the ledge while dipping his head and one shoulder through, his advancement stopped. The man's struggle to get completely through the opening became panicked.

A long wooden stick sliced through the light and began striking the lodged man.

With his face outside the room, his cries of pain were barely heard. He was struck many times on his buttocks and lower back and his faint screams became gargled and choked. Eventually, blood diluted by rain dripped off the man's wounds, adding to the puddle forming under the opening's ledge.

Thrusting himself forward, he desperately tried to get through the opening and out of range of the stick viciously striking his backside, but he was just too big.

Chapter 32

Jason surveyed the window; it was much narrower in width than in height because the man would have fit through had he not been so wide across the shoulders, chest and belly. After a painful period, in which the man actively tried to compress himself, he finally collapsed at the base of the window - one-third of his body getting drenched outside while the other, beaten to a pulp, went limp inside the room.

He had not only absorbed an awful beating but nearly crushed himself attempting to squeeze through the too-small opening.

The stick swung one more time, striking a body no longer reacting to the impact. Hands reached out, grabbed the man and pulled him back into the darkness. There was a struggle; loud, excited voices beckoned other men to rush over, their backs the only thing visible through the light. The commotion culminated with a ripping sound. And, soon after, quiet.

A topless man with blood smeared over his chest walked through the light in Jason's direction. Chains chinked nearby when the two men tethered with him moved. Prompted by a tug at his arms, his body walked toward the rear. They were led through the light to a back wall, where that thick, heavy chain was fed through the large round link at the cross-section of the chains connecting each man's ankle and wrist cuffs.

As the first man was pushed toward the window that heavy chain resisted his advance as he labored physically under its weight.

Of interest was the pile off in the corner. A clear view revealed it consisted of bodies – corpses stacked waist high. Lifeless limbs - arms and legs - protruded out from the mound. His head snapped away from that sight and for that he was thankful.

Staring back through the glassless window, his new position offered a straight-on view. Jason saw huge raindrops falling. They looked much larger than normal. He saw the sea and a narrow slice of the horizon just beneath the top edge of the window. A dark sky sandwiched between milk-white clouds and a shimmering body of water. Waves crashed against huge, uneven boulders lining the shore and sea water sprayed in the air from the impact.

The first of his troika continued his march, eventually eclipsing most of the light from the window. He arched his back and angled his head through the window while turning his body, searching for a way out. His hips were caught in the width of the opening; he had not held his turn long enough to slide through completely sideways.

He turned his chest around too soon and had in effect wedged himself in the opening. After a strike from that wielded stick, he twisted around and propelled himself through the window with one foot.

Jason stepped up a couple paces. Able to see the lower portion now, there was a long line of men walking away in a line through a four-foot, boulder-lined trench. People – their head and shoulders the only part visible – walked out about 30 yards within the canal as it wound out of sight. The migration was steady, involving 20, maybe 30 people. Their pace was very slow.

The second man – who had been standing next to him in the stairwell – began his walk toward the window. He had more trouble lifting the heavy chain than getting through the window.

A hand grabbed Jason's segment of chain and he was directed toward the window. When he got to the light, the hand released. In the periphery of his vision that wooden stick rose in the air through the light and into the elevated shadows. He walked toward the window - a window that was so narrow Jason doubted if any good-sized man could fit through.

Closer to the opening, he saw the clouds churning above the blackened sky. They were extremely bright yet there was something even brighter above them. Jason could not imagine the moon ever being so large and bright.

That bright object was the source of the beam of light that sliced through the room.

Working the new heavier chain through the cross-sectioned o-ring and between his legs, a bewildered Jason looked on in awe at his body working to advance to the window. He was amazed there was no physicality perceived from such effort. It was, however, only a passing thought, as he stepped closer, for he became mesmerized by the view through the opening.

The milky white clouds were moving rapidly in a circular motion as waves crashed the shore more violently. Lightning flashed in the distance, yet Jason had not heard thunder. At the base of the window, he saw that the heavy chain led from the room, up over the window ledge, then dropped down to a landing, across a short rocky path, and into the canal. Huge rain droplets, driven by a gale, pelted the area - and, the people walking through the rocky ditch.

His left leg rose and his foot planted on the rain-soaked sill. Leaning forward, he stuck his head and shoulder out the window. Drenched by the rain, he was no longer surprised at not feeling the effects. With head down, chin to his chest, he could hear his voice vocalizing the strain of trying to fit through the narrow opening.

Only partially through, his forward progress stopped and seconds later he heard a loud thwap as his voice yelled out in an agonized pitch fraught with pain. That raised stick must have struck him and his body reacted, though he had not felt it.

More importantly, he was certain he was stuck in the opening.

Chapter 33

Jason had seen how other men made it through. They twisted their body and slithered through vertically. But without control of his body, how could he manage it?

While pinned in the exit, he became aware of two scars on his knee, which had been lifted to the windowsill. There was a rough circular welt healing poorly with a bumpy, caked-on scab. And just underneath, a crescent shaped abrasion still red in the middle, but healing smoothly around the edges.

Thinking back to when he was a child at Spencer Elementary School, he remembered he had injured himself falling on a gravel-covered playground. His scars were exactly like these, except his had healed years ago, or so he thought. The sight of those scars made Jason feel a direct connection to this uncooperative body. A sense of mutual survival took over his psyche.

That stick struck him again and this time his face shot up, followed by a yell so steeped in agony his brain shuddered. Rain spattered around his face, affecting his vision and causing his eyes to squint. With his head up, the brightly shining object above the clouds began to have an effect on him.

It was huge - much larger than the sun, the moon or any other heavenly body in earth's sky. Jason perceived warmth coming from that light. He was not sure how or where the warmth was felt because he had not sensed any feeling whatsoever in any of these surroundings. Still, the warmth from the celestial light was there – somewhere - and it encouraged him.

He tried to yell out, "We still have to twist," but his voice only echoed within the vestiges of his mind. Then his head dropped down, suggesting he was defeated and on the verge of giving up. The warmth from that heavenly light was gone as soon as his head fell.

Panic percolated in Jason's mind.

He had already discovered he had no direct control over his body and that meant his vocal chords and his ability to speak were not at his command. However, when his mind sent instruction to speak, he could hear his words in his mind. Thinking maybe – just maybe – his body could hear those thoughts as they reverberated through his head, he concentrated on sending more specific counsel echoing through his brain:

"Don't give up – We have to turn our body – We can get through – We must twist to the side – We must turn sideways."

Thwap! He was hit again and his head snapped up, accompanied by an extended, blood-curdling yell. That internal warmth from the light resumed - and intensified. It could only be felt when his head faced upwards. Deducing that if he could feel the warmth with his head to the sky, suggesting a physical connection, Jason thought perhaps at that time his body could hear his pleas to turn.

Despite the rain and the discomfort, Jason believed it was vitally important for his body to keep its head up. He thought, "It's now or never." Another strike and the high volume of his body's yelling forced him to raise the decibel of his internal call. In his mind, the commanding words boomed:

"Twist your body – turn your body."

At the height of the yell, his body began to turn. Twisting slowly, Jason saw that he was beginning to extend further and further out. As he inched forward, he registered a new, stranger sensation. That perceived warmth from the celestial light expanded into a pressure, a strong invisible force that pulled on him.

A gentle swooshing sound whistled in his ears as he slipped through the window. Jason quickly realized this different force was not pulling him down but was in fact pulling him up. Meanwhile, gravity took something to the landing, but it was not him.

His view changed rapidly. The unfelt raindrops, once falling on his body and spattering back up, were now falling by close together. It was as if they were falling through him. He could see downward but he was moving up and out diagonally in the direction of the sea.

When he elevated past the edge of the building's seaside wall he was stunned to see a large ship with scores – maybe hundreds - of people on the deck.

They were being huddled to the stern of the ship where they were stepping down to the hull. They were all Africans about to make the trans-Atlantic voyage across the Middle Passage. That canal, full of men slowly walking away from the building, wrapped around and deposited its occupants right at the shore, along with a river of flowing rainwater. The massive chain put through the o-ring went all the way through, making the trek extremely difficult for those still in the canal.

Gliding over the shore, Jason saw smaller boats ferrying the people out to the ship. A few boats currently in route were overloaded, being tossed about by the waves and inclement weather.

The latest group of three men began walking down the rocky path and into the canal. That third man looked just like him.

His ascending speed accelerated as Jason saw the surrounding area shrinking fast in his sight.

It was too much for him. Not able to hold on; he passed out.

High Ground View of the Women Courtyard

Death Room at El Mina by Ferris Shelton 1998

Ferris and Nana Esi at El Mina 1998

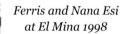

A Library for Children at El Mina by Janice Mazzallo 2018

Saturday

The Reflection

Chapter 34

Daybreak arrived with Callie wide awake in her bed.

Having tossed and turned most of night, her sleep occurred in two-hour durations, broken by short intervals of remorse. By six o'clock she gave up all hope of falling back to sleep. Looking over at Jason, he was apparently fast asleep, sprawled across the other side of the bed. Thankfully he was calm, in stark contrast to the way she had seen him the morning before.

She considered waking him, but opted against it as he seemed to be resting comfortably. Contrary to the way she felt, he looked at peace. He had suffered so much recently, and Callie felt sorry for him - believing him to be her soul mate; as he suffered, so she now suffered.

Stressed beyond distraction, Callie got out of bed, nervous energy fueling every step. She put the bedroom in order as the nuances of their relationship took center stage in her mind.

Though Jason believed otherwise, she had known of him from the time she was a young girl. She remembers that as a boy he possessed an oversized head and a wide face. Her first remembrance of him was in third grade, for he was one of the boys in the back of the class who wrestled all day, never bothering to pay attention and never forced to either. They were basically ignored by the teacher and tolerated by the rest of the class.

However, back in the day, every so often, he would show up in some memorable part of her youth. When her family moved to a better neighborhood, she saw Jason walking around on more than a few occasions with Michael Fisher and Allen Cosby - two guys she would later meet while in high school.

She and Jason's encounters were always by chance because he rode a bus to a school far away from their neighborhood.

One summer when she was 12 or 13, they sat next to each other on a roller coaster ride at the Great America amusement park near Chicago. By then, Jason had added glasses to his big head and fat face. At the time, he wasn't anything special and she saw no reason to reach out to him with conversation.

Pausing to look at his reflection in the mirror, she wondered what was happening in his sleep. During the times she'd awakened in the middle of the night and checked on Jason's condition, he had lain on his back sweating, though not nearly as profusely as the past few nights.

Mostly, his sleep was uneventful except for one instance when he grunted, mumbling under his breath. Sometime after midnight, Jason's body was turned awkwardly. Yet, at that time, he was sound asleep.

Resisting the temptation to wake Jason, Callie went downstairs to begin her day. It was 7:45 when she walked into the kitchen, beginning a breakfast. While whisking the pancake batter, Callie thought how wonderful her life had been.

After that roller coaster ride, she had not seen Jason again until a party at a friend's house nine or 10 years later - on her 21st birthday. Jason had a military haircut and had grown into his head and face.

When he entered the party, she recognized him right away and thought him to be quite handsome. After finally making eye contact, she realized he had no idea who she was. Perhaps she had grown into herself as well. Over the years, she kept quiet and allowed him to believe that was their first meeting.

He seemed so enamored with the irony of living in the same part of Chicago and never meeting that she could not bring herself to ruin it for him.

One of their early dates was to attend a baseball game. He was a huge fan but it was a sport she found to be unrelentingly boring, though he claimed there was always some subtle action going on. This particular game started later than usual and he was visibly embarrassed.

However, the delay was fine with her because she wanted to get to know him and was not that interested in seeing a bunch of men running around spitting and scratching themselves.

A quaint smile made its way through mounting angst while she reminisced:

"Attention ladies and gentlemen, today's game will start at 3:30 p.m. to accommodate the national audience. We apologize for any inconvenience," announced the stadium PA system.

"What - 3:30! Shit, I thought the game was starting at the regular time. No wonder we got that parking spot," stated Jason, nervously pulling at everything in his pockets, looking for the ticket stubs.

"What time was it supposed to start?" asked Callie.

"I should have known - there's no one here. The place is not even half-full." He found the stubs but seemed satisfied with just that, for no matter what time the game was to start, a different time was set.

"I thought you said the park would be full and noisy."

"It will be - at 3:30. Now we'll have to wait three fuckin' hours."

"Jason, don't cuss like that - it's not necessary." She grabbed his hand and felt the thick veins stretching throughout. "If you went to church with me you'd learn that."

"Oh, I'm sorry Callie, you're right, I won't swear so much." Jason made a "duh" sound and patted his forehead as if to keep in mind something he already knew to remember. "What church do you go to? I'd like to go with you."

"I'd love for you to come with me tomorrow. I'll call you in the morning." A test passed, thought Callie, "I think you'll enjoy it."

"I know I will. And you're going to enjoy this game today," agreed Jason. "I can't believe you've never been to Wrigley Field. I love baseball. I played through my sophomore year in high school."

"Why'd you stop?"

"Well, I didn't. During my junior year, I didn't make varsity because of a stupid choice I made."

"Your choice was not to play baseball?"

"It may as well have been. At the time, looking good for the girls at my high school was more important. So, you know what I did - I stopped wearing my glasses because I thought they would think I was better looking without them."

"And...," Callie looked confused. "What did that have to do with baseball?"

"Later on, I came to realize, without my glasses, I couldn't see the curveball pitches as well. I started striking out - a lot! So, I got cut from the team. And you know what? It was such a stupid thing to do; God, I was so not ready back then. I couldn't hit pitches I used to crush. I didn't make varsity when, the year before, I was one of the best junior varsity players. And, wouldn't you know, I still didn't get a girlfriend."

"Now, that's striking out."

"Yeah right." Jason smiled, leaning into her just a bit, to softly add, "I swore not to ever allow something like that to happen to me again. You know, to sell myself out. So, I don't try to be cool because that's not me. And I don't try to hide my intelligence anymore. I like to read and I'm determined to complete college and go on to succeed in business."

"So no more taking off your glasses to impress the girls, uh?" Callie asked as she pushed him away in mock seriousness.

"Well yeah, I mean, no, I mean...Callie you don't like my glasses?"

"I like you fine, Jason," responded Callie, smiling.

"Even if I looked like this?"

Jason took off his glasses and crossed his eyes. Laughing out loud, Callie tried to hide from the look by using his shoulder as a shield. "That's not funny, Jason!"

"Okay, Callie," grinned Jason, reaching an arm around her shoulder.

Settling into the hug, without looking up, Callie said, "And I would never ask you not to wear them if you need them."

"It's established that I can't see a curveball without them."

"Keep 'em on then, in case life throws you a curveball or two. They fit you and I think they make you look smart."

"You mean they make me look like a nerd?"

"I didn't say that," she said sitting up abruptly.

"I'm just kidding," Jason said, gently pulling her back down and putting on his glasses. "But it's tough in Chicago. I've always been different. Even now, I want to do different things with my life. I don't want to just eke out an existence, scraping by on the margins - I want to be rich, by legal means, of course. Since I was discharged from the Marine Corps, I've been working on my accounting degree so I can be a businessman. I haven't met many on Lockwood striving for that."

"If that's your dream, Jason, go for it. Be true to yourself."

"You're right - that's why I wear my glasses, now."

Following a few moments of silence, Jason offered, "Hey, there's the hot dog vendor. Do you want something to eat? Wrigley Field hot dogs are the best."

Thankful for the change of topic, Callie replied, "Yes, and can you get me a pop, too?"

"Yeah sure, it doesn't look like he's coming this way. I'll go down to him." Jason stood and galloped down the aisle to the concession man.

"What a guy," thought Callie. She had long ago decided not to settle for a man with poor character - a decision that had left her mostly alone in recent times. At that point in time, she had recently stopped dating a guy from church because he was not really doing it for her.

He had a nasal-sounding voice and groomed himself in such a way that she felt awkward when with him, as if she needed to keep up. He wore the curl of the day and his hair was always perfect. When he began having manicures and pedicures, she knew he was all wrong for her.

Jason was a man, but not typical of the men masquerading at the time as prospects. She couldn't remember the black male come-on of the day, but whatever it was, Jason wasn't it. Callie was getting caught-up, but nevertheless tried not to lead with her heart. During this early period, Jason exhibited patience, persistence, and a real passion for life.

Yep, she was falling in love. Compared to her other choices, Jason was nearly too right to be real.

Her body tingled, starting at the base of her neck and running down her spine, almost every time they were to meet. His presence was felt before he was on the stadium seat next to her. Whew, Jason was definitely doing it for her.

"Here you go. I hope orange soda is okay. I mean orange pop. I think Chicago is the only place in the country where people call soda, 'pop.'"

"It's also the only place in the country where we are right now."

Jason laughed and handed over her meal. Just as they were finishing, he asked, "Do you want to walk around the park? It's early still, we can probably get close to the dugout."

"The dugout? Oh, now that sounds exciting."

"Okay, Ms. Smartypants. This being your first game, we're going to make it special - you'll never forget today, Callie."

She loved the way he spoke her name. She was never "Baby," "Shorty," or some other overused shorthand term for a nickname.

They went over to the Cubs' dugout, where Jason had a brief conversation with one of the players by the name of Leon Durham. He threw up an autographed baseball and you would have thought Jason won the lottery. He tossed the ball in air as they walked through Wrigley Field, being careful not to let it hit the ground. Half-way around, they had to wade through the many, many people arriving at the park.

She felt safe and alive as they walked arm-in-arm, talking and laughing.

"Welcome to Wrigley Field, home of the Chicago Cubs. Today's starting lineups are..."

By the time they returned to their seats, the ballpark had filled and an energized buzz infected the once quiet and desolate stands. After the National Anthem, the PA system announcements were loud, forcing them to nearly shout.

"Callie, the game is about to start. I'm really sorry I didn't hear about the time change earlier. I hate changes and surprises, but we had fun anyway, didn't we?"

"Oh Jason, I loved our talk. We made the best of the time. Besides, on your way to being a big businessman everything may not work out as planned or as you'd like."

"Which is why I'm getting prepared; I'm studying business and focused on doing a good job at work. I'll be ready for anything. But, what about you? What's your goal in life?"

"My goal?" There was an even louder roar from the crowd as the players took the field.

"Yes Callie, what do you want out of life?"

"I want to be happy."

"What?" replied Jason standing to his feet, hands-clapping.

"I want to be happy," shouted Callie as she stood-up.

"Happy!" exclaimed Jason, looking for something more. "Everybody wants happiness, Callie. But what if you're already happy? Isn't there something more than that?"

"Yes, of course," said Callie. She clutched his arm, and reached her mouth close to his ear. "My mission in life is to go to Heaven."

"Go to Heaven?" He put his arm around her waist. "Well, I want to go there with you, but we may as well live rich until we get there."

"Rich is good, Jason. But, being a person that earns a place in Heaven is better."

The public-address system blared, *"Play Ball."*

Callie's smile faded as her thoughts returned to the task of completing breakfast.

She remembered how articulate and charming Jason was that day. She could listen to him talk about something as dry as baseball and still be interested. His team – the Chicago Cubs – won that day and he exulted in emotional joy. The sight had her thinking: "Here is a man that does not try to conceal his feelings."

This trait, along with others, led Callie to fall deeply in love with Jason. He was a good and decent man. She was sure of it then and even surer now.

Chapter 35

Living in Chicago allowed their union to weather the turbulent early years. Though they were private people, there were times when having both extended families nearby helped smooth over a few rough edges. Their biggest disagreement happened five years ago when he was offered a supervisor position in Atlanta, Georgia. Initially she did not want to move away from the family, but finally changed her mind to be supportive of his career ambitions.

Now, she believed that ambition to be insatiable, as it devoured other aspects of their lives. Still, the relocation to Atlanta had been good for them. After they moved, Jason insisted on selling her car to save money to buy their first home. She had not liked that idea, arguing against it.

However, going without a car for six months prior to buying their first home in Decatur was now a minor sacrifice. Plus, within a few months, she had a nicer car. Callie loved their house and was extremely annoyed when Jason wanted to sell it to buy a different, more expensive home in Stone Mountain. She pushed against the move but eventually gave in to Jason's argument. And yes, that had worked out well, too. Their home in Stone Mountain was a dream and she was proud of it.

She prepared her plate, but her unsettled stomach was not meshing well with her preoccupied mind and she only picked over her meal. Before leaving the kitchen, Callie prepared a hearty plate for Jason and put it in the microwave.

The next hour was spent cleaning the dining room and living room with gospel music playing softly in the background. Performing these duties by rote, her thinking process was left to negotiate a self-induced labyrinth. Callie was stretching herself thin, attempting to simultaneously think down two paths. She wanted him to change, but not too much.

Sure, she considered his ambition to be selfish at times, but it was a nuisance in an otherwise solid marriage, for she loved this man dearly. That love and his current condition had her feeling mixed emotions about the pressure she had him under lately. She wanted to have a baby and had grown outwardly weary of his insistence that they wait. Jason was unwilling to compromise on this issue.

And she did not like it.

As far as she was concerned, they had waited seven years. She had wanted a child since their newlywed year; since he promised they would start a family if she agreed to move to Atlanta; since the last excuse of waiting until the next promotion.

Well, he was promoted in March yet still resisted the idea of starting a family. The newest reasons were no longer of interest to her. She was not okay with his delay tactics and was making sure he knew it.

There were moments when a strong maternal instinct would tempt her to throw the birth control pills out and let Mother Nature take its course, but she preferred to have her husband's blessing.

Even with her recent change in attitude, she was not sure if he really understood the depths of her frustration. More and more he obsessed about work and his job. When they first arrived in the South they spent almost all their time together; just the two of them driving around lost for hours in metropolitan Atlanta, getting to know their new area.

But recently, she could not get him to take her anyplace. He was either too tired from working or had to rest so he could get to work early the next day.

They were spending less and less time together and he was spending more and more time working, leaving her at home. She did not like that either. Callie was beginning to feel like a business widow. Sure, she had the church, and she loved working in the auxiliary committees and singing in the choir, but she wanted her husband back.

While vacuuming, she hoped the noise would disturb Jason enough to wake him. With this in mind, she spent extra time on the foyer and entrance to the stairs leading up to the bedrooms. When the appliance was put back in the closet, she turned off the radio, listening for any sound upstairs.

Hearing nothing, she went back to the kitchen to inventory their grocery needs with her mind in overdrive. The dreams were wearing Jason down and she worried about his health. When Kenny Mendes said his system was laboring and his vital signs weakening, it validated what she had seen the past few days.

The clock on the wall chimed the top of the hour, as it does every hour, yet this time the usual sound caused her to nearly jump out of her skin. Trying not to get too worked up, Callie switched her thoughts to the Bible verse. It stated that in seven days the wounds would be healed. Thinking to herself, "This is the seventh day," she breathed a sigh of relief.

Seconds later, that same thought brought on another wave of worry. This was indeed the seventh day, but he had not risen from the sixth night.

She compiled her list for the grocery store and went back upstairs to the bedroom. Jason had not moved, despite the noise of the vacuum cleaner. Walking across the room to her dresser, she grabbed a scarf from her drawer and stood in front of the mirror.

She covered her hair while wrestling with the temptation to wake him, eventually succumbing to the strength of that yearning.

Turning toward the bed, Callie bent down without actually touching him and whispered, "Jason your breakfast is in the microwave...Jason?...Jason?"

There was no response. He did not move, but she saw he was breathing as his back raised and lowered regularly and effortlessly. Callie closed her eyes and silently scolded herself for the motive of checking on him in the first place. She wanted to make sure he was all right but just as pressing an impetus was appeasing her own personal anxiety. That anxiety eased only superficially for she considered he might still be in the middle of a dream.

Writing a note stating she was out grocery shopping, Callie nervously tucked her hair into the scarf, grabbed her purse and left the room. Back downstairs, she tried to force herself to relax but was having little success not thinking about Jason. All kinds of thoughts were swirling in her head. Callie felt as though she were being gently pricked anytime she moved, as if surrounded by pins and needles.

When leaving the house, she satisfied herself that he would surely be up when she returned.

At her car, she decided to run a couple of other errands. Along with doing the grocery shopping, there was a need for stamps from the post office and to stop by the church to pick up the Sunday morning program information that she printed every week. It was 9:30 and Callie would be away from the house for more than an hour, but Jason was never far from her thoughts.

She drove to the neighborhood plaza where the post office and grocery store were located. While waiting for stamps, Callie felt justified at being angry with Jason, but sorry for the way she had been expressing it. Good two-way communication was the cornerstone of their marriage and they talked about everything.

Callie believed Jason did not just hear her when she talked – but that he actually listened.

And he often shared his feelings with her in ways that reinforced their bond – and their love had grown over the years because of this. But that was all changing. Starting a family and his blind ambition aside, these recent dreams were the most troubling evidence of that change. After mailing a few bills and buying stamps, she left the post office and walked to Kroger's grocery store.

Wheeling her cart through the aisles, thinking how she had been hurt and disappointed at the meeting with Kenny and Dr. Caswell, she realized that her hurt centered on being unaware of all the things Jason was going through.

He had not told her much about the dreams. He had not even mentioned them until Wednesday morning, the day she found him shouting in the kitchen. Before that, all she knew was that he had a simple nightmare Tuesday night.

She not only had a right to know, but to know way before the boom was lowered at a meeting with others. Still, the knife cut both ways. Callie had also been embarrassed for Jason to find out that she had discussed their family business in personal detail with Kenny before the two of them had seriously talked about it. When Kenny called her after speaking with Jason, she felt he needed to know more than Jason would tell.

Callie stood in the grocery check-out line battling competing thoughts - there had never been many secrets between them. Was he pushing her away? Was she pushing him away? Were they both pushing? There were too many questions with too few answers. Her scattered mind kept coming back to the one big thing that bothered her the most.

She left the store, packed the groceries in the trunk, and drove to her church. On her way to pick-up Sunday's morning service program a weight on her conscious was becoming difficult to carry.

Chapter 36

At the church, Callie walked through the sanctuary, stopping momentarily to say a prayer for Jason. Kneeling before the alter and fighting back a sense of sorrow that had steadily gained on her the past couple of days; she closed her eyes, bowing her head. Being a spiritual person, she wondered in meditation, "Have I used my blessing as a weapon against the man I love?"

Leaping to her feet, Callie hurriedly left the church, without even checking on the status of the programs. She drove home, speeding with worry, nervously pondering a little secret that had grown too big to ignore.

On Thursday, when Dr. Caswell asked about the argument Sunday night, insinuating something may have triggered the dreams, she became suspicious. Later on she felt terrible after reviewing the entire episode during the drive home from Clay Calhoun's party. A feeling of personal responsibility for the recent events was born and she had silently carried a burden of guilt ever since.

She feared that perhaps she had unleashed these dreams. She had been upset with Jason for the way he acted at the party Sunday. She had been upset with Jason for his continuing reluctance to have a child. She had been upset with Jason for focusing too much on work to the detriment of their marriage and relationship. When he pulled to the side of the road Sunday night, she tuned him out.

All his shouting might as well have occurred with him in the car alone because she was not listening. If he had known what she was thinking, he would have really gotten mad. While he yelled away, she closed her eyes and asked God to intercede.

Callie prayed for Jason to change - to diminish the cold, dispassionate ambition dominating his life and to build a stronger sense of family; to deliver him from passive acceptance of things he had to know were wrong for the sake of his own personal gain; to have him be more the man she knew him to be.

She had forgotten about that prayer until Thursday. That's when she learned that the traumatic dreams began Sunday night and immediately perceived spiritual undertones to the bizarre things happening since.

When Jason remembered the word in the vision her intuition led her to check the Bible. She found nothing that night but Friday morning, after seeing the stress of Jason' sleep, that intuition was even stronger.

When reaching for her grandmother's old Bible her hands quivered so she nearly dropped it from the mantel. By the time she sat down and turned to the concordance in the back, there were goose bumps over her entire body. When she found that word, translated from Hebrew, pointing to a specific passage in the Bible, she was excited that she might have helped Jason understand the dreams, yet on edge that her private prayer could have been their root cause.

Turning into their subdivision, her nerves were becoming unstrung, thinking she may have triggered these tough, tense times for her husband and herself. Pulling into the driveway, Callie had worked herself into a tizzy and now needed to regain her composure. Grabbing the groceries, she looked up at the bedroom window but could not tell if the light was on.

Stepping through the front door, Callie called upstairs, "Jason, groceries." Waiting in the foyer for a few seconds, she did not hear any noise that would indicate he was awake. A quick look around the main floor also showed no sign that he had come down. Again she called upstairs, "Jason, you gonna help me with the groceries?"

Standing still, listening for a response, she heard nothing. Callie reflexively looked at her watch again – it was almost eleven o'clock. Though Jason sometimes slept in on Saturday, never did he sleep this late.

That was it. That was the exact moment when she decided she had waited long enough. Jason would just have to wake up – and wake up right now.

She put the bags down as a strangling uneasiness harnessed her every move. Walking upstairs, clutching the banister, oppressed by the accumulated angst of a day that had frazzled her last nerve, she slowly opened the door and timidly crept into the room. It was as if her intentions were other than to wake him.

Jason seemed too still. Fearful of touching him, Callie walked over to his side of the bed and called out in a vibrato-laden voice,

"Ja-Ja-Jason, wake-up. Ja-Ja-Jason."

He did not move but took a deep breath.

"Ja-Jason, will you please wake up?" Callie pleaded.

"Woman, can't you see I'm sleeping?" Jason said, face down on the pillow.

Relieved at hearing his voice, Callie asked, "How you doin', honey? I was getting kinda worried."

"Oh Callie, you worry too much," responded Jason, turning over. "That's why I don't tell you everything."

"Oh really. Well, you gonna sleep all day?"

"I don't know, why? What time is it?"

"It's eleven o'clock"

"Eleven o'clock!" Surprised, Jason rolled over and sat up. He stretched through a yawn and huffed, "I didn't know it was that late."

"How long have you been awake? I've been up here a couple of times and…"

"Oh, I heard you. I woke up before you this morning. I was so relieved at waking from sound sleep and not from one of those dreams that I couldn't believe it. So I fluffed my pillow and went back to sleep – you know - to test it again, but later I had a horrible dream."

"Wait, you dreamed after you woke-up this morning?"

"Yeah, that my wife left a vacuum cleaner running right outside the door."

"Ha, ha, ha. So, you were awake all the time."

"Off and on."

"Then you didn't have a dream last night?"

"Oh yeah, I did. But it was over before I woke up. For the first time this week, I wasn't scared awake by a dream."

Together they went downstairs and talked over the week-long ordeal. Jason told Callie of the dream, mentioning how right at the very end he felt a connection with the man with whom he shared a body in the dreams and that their individual beings eventually united in the effort to get through the "door of no return."

Epilogue
The El Mina Slave Castle

Chapter 37

The dreams fostered change, the details of which would play out over future months.

The profound experience affected Jason's life in many ways. He did not become abruptly hypersensitive but rather established well-defined boundaries. Bob Farrington's antics were politely and respectfully dissuaded. Far more importantly, in addition to no longer tolerating slights on African-Americans, he now spoke up against mean-spirited jokes of any kind. Jason felt ashamed for the way he had acted over the years.

Despite his education and opportunity, he realized he had a shared historical experience with all African-Americans and would never again look upon his heritage with anything other than reverence.

This conviction would not lesson his pride in being American, but would strengthen it. In this land of immigrants, Italian-Americans were proud of their Italian roots; Korean-Americans still felt a connection to Korea; all other nationalities in America's melting pot were proud of their origins.

The 'Old World' connection was severed when Africans arrived in this hemisphere – customs and culture lost by the force of man's will. But thankfully, the human spirit is not beholden to the whims of men.

The experience made clear he knew very little about Africa. And until that seven-day period, he had not thought it important to be even moderately interested. But the dreams and the *El Mina* slave castle changed that.

If Europe had Spanish, German, and English people and Asia had a mix of people from nations such as India, China, and those of the Middle East, then Africa, the other 'Old World' continent, could not be a homogeneous collection of people without any ethnic differences; to be identified solely on the darkness of their skin.

The African - his host in the dreams - was an African, yes, and a Ghanaian maybe, but he was more than just those broader terms – he was Ashanti. That was his ethnicity - a specific, distinctive people on the continent of Africa with a language, customs, and culture that make them unique – as unique as the French or the Japanese.

Jason had not learned much about Africa in school. That lack of formal learning would not, in and of itself, be enough for him to deny his African origins. He had also been influenced by America's portrayals of Africa in the media and general culture. Most impressions perpetuated stereotypes of Africa being a vast, violent, and backward wasteland. His research revealed a continent of beautiful beaches and temperate climates, rich in raw materials, agriculture, and precious metals.

Africa is also a continent made up of over 50 countries full of diverse people and wildlife, and containing some of nature's more beautiful and pristine areas. It is essentially not unlike other places on earth. There were certainly remote areas with people living in the bush and existing as they had for perhaps centuries, maybe even millennia. But Africa also has many bustling urban centers with all the usual institutions and infrastructure one would find in modern western areas – museums, banks, organized sports, colleges, and universities.

After the final dream, he sought every opportunity to converse with people recently arriving from Africa. The Atlanta area has a large close-knit community of African immigrants.

He inquired about their homeland - his Motherland - and almost unanimously, their opinion was that Africa was a poor but mostly a happy place.

Yes, his outlook changed forever. Thus, what was once out of alignment was properly realigned.

He endeavored to learn more about Africa, though not through the filter of the American media but through his own effort and research.

Knowledge is useless when contained within oneself; it's what one does with it that gives it life.

He had always believed in lifelong learning, but in this case he was not so much learning as catching up with the humor, language, and etiquette-related nuances of his community. Moses of the Bible grew-up within the Pharaoh's opulence yet after discovering he was not Egyptian royalty, he did not have to learn to be Hebrew.

Jason chose to accept himself; allowing innate instincts to replace conditioned behavior, learning that one cannot outgrow one's history.

He discovered heritage is the still water that runs deepest.

That Saturday evening Callie came close to telling Jason about her prayer on Sunday night. She decided to wait a few days to see if the dreams ended and to see if he would truly change, because to change is one thing and sometimes to change positively is something entirely different. In the days and weeks that followed, she saw change for the better.

To this day she has never told him, believing that her prayer that angry Sunday night was answered.

Wanda Rodger's employment at Edwards started that following Monday morning and in a matter of months she flawlessly ran accounts payable. Jason's A/P responsibility consisted of reviewing totals and managing the month-end close out. They worked very well together and developed a good professional relationship.

Her Jamaican accent became an enjoyable, interesting element of the workday and certainly not a hindrance to business.

In early November Callie was informed she was pregnant. That made her extra happy - and hyperactive. Within a month, the spare bedroom upstairs in their home was completely redecorated in the motif of a baby's nursery. It was finished just as she was beginning to show. During the early weeks of the pregnancy the initial stages of fundamental change took root in their marital relationship as Jason assumed more household duties, thus was home more.

He did not let on as much as Callie, but he too was excited about having a baby.

A lot of his happiness was derived from her. Specifically, with Callie pregnant, he noticed her in ways he had when they were first dating. The life gestating inside made her skin radiant and that unique spirit of hers irresistible.

She was back to that beautiful person, inside and out, that he fell in love with years ago. The pregnancy helped rekindle the attentiveness of a relationship that had lost its edge.

Chapter 38

Later that year, over the Christmas holiday season, Jason and Callie planned to fly to Ghana for vacation. They had scheduled the vacation prior to learning she was with child. Upon finding out, Jason had insisted on canceling the trip and had not relented until Kenny Mendes told him that taking a flight in the first or second trimester was statistically safer than driving a car.

The day before they were to travel, Jason stopped by Just Add Honey, to speak with Judy. The first thing he noticed as he opened the door - there was no chime. It threw him off. He looked at the door jamb, where the chime alarm had been, but there was no evidence of one ever having been there.

Looking around, he did not see Judy or Sophia. He asked a man standing at the counter if Judy was around. He claimed to have never heard of Judy or for that matter Sophia, either. He said there weren't any older people working there, that he only hired Georgia State students. After a brief dispute, the man said he owns the store and should know who works for him.

The 14-hour flight to Africa was fraught with suspense and excitement. They decided to fly directly, choosing Ghana Airways, instead of traveling to Europe and catching a connecting flight.

Callie and Jason found Ghana to be a marvelous, safe, and beautiful country. Everywhere they went people greeted them with large, genuine smiles. *"Akwaaba,"* the local word for "welcome" was heard at every stop. There was a friendly respect extended from the locals, even off the usual tourist path, that is not always encountered by Americans in a foreign country.

The artwork in Ghana was incredible. Jason and Callie gave away clothes and other items to free up a suitcase to bring as many of the beautiful crafts home as possible. This was one time when he was glad his wife over packed.

Her reluctance to part with some of her personal items disappeared as the show of genuine appreciation by the Ghanaians for jeans, t-shirts, and sandals tugged at her heart.

They were also pleasantly surprised that most of the people spoke fairly good English, though with a heavy British accent. The Ghanaians had, by African-American standards, a proper way of enunciating words, using "Queen's English" diction.

Jason thought it ironic that people some Americans considered of marginal intelligence were almost all tri-lingual, speaking English and at least two African languages.

There were a number of ethnic groups, or what are considered tribes, in Ghana: Akan, Ewe, and Ga were all different people united by a common dialect allowing cross communication. That dialect was Twi. The local languages were spoken with an aggressive emphatic tone, but this was very misleading for it was merely the linguistic style. During their stay in Ghana, Jason and Callie did not see anything remotely resembling anger or violence.

The day after Christmas they took a boat ride from a tourist resort area near the Akosombo Dam on the Volta River, the major river waterway in Ghana. There was a band playing, a good meal served, and a lively party on board. On the return trip to their hotel in Accra, the capitol of Ghana, their driver requested to stop in his home village, a place called Mepe. They agreed, after the driver assured them it was just off the main road and not much of a detour.

Mepe was a small village with no electricity or plumbing. Jason was fascinated, for this was truly the bush. There happened to be a celebration that day and a meeting of local chiefs. After being told there were African-Americans in their village, the chiefs asked to meet them. Jason and Callie walked down a dirt path lined with small vegetable patches, thatch and mud huts, and people looking at them with amused curiosity.

The elder chief, sitting in a hand-carved, decorated chair invited them onto an open-air platform in the middle of the village and explained he was a fifth-generation leader. Jason calculated the birth of the first chief in that lineage to be in the 1800s.

After a libation, which turned out to be peppermint schnapps, he asked to which tribe Jason and Callie belonged. Of course, they had no idea. The elder chief told him, based on the shape of his head, his facial construction and body frame; he was most likely a Fanti, a subset of the Akan people and a close cousin of the Ashanti. All the other chiefs on the platform agreed.

There was less agreement when attempting to assess Callie's tribal ancestry, though the elder chief said she was most likely part Ga. He stated that other non-African influences made her ethnicity difficult to know positively.

When they resumed the ride back to Accra, Jason thought the firm opinion that he looked like a Fanti was in keeping with the assumed Ashanti origins of his host in the dreams. He suspected, as that mysterious Judy said, that that person was an ancestor. Now, with the chief's independent assessment, he was even more certain.

On New Year's Eve they went on a tour of the Ghanaian slave castles. There are a number of forts and castles on the coast of Ghana, which is located just above the Equator. The weather was beautiful that day. The morning of the tour, Jason was in a pensive mood, not sure what to expect. Callie, on the other hand, was jovial and playful in her attempt to help him relax and enjoy the trip.

She commented on every interesting sight along the route as they traveled from Accra to the seaside port of Cape Coast, from the people in rice fields working topless to the markets and shopping areas jammed with people. She marveled at the women walking with baskets and other items perfectly balanced on their heads and the men shepherding their goat or cattle herds. Her mood was carefree.

However, she was only moderately successful at exporting that lightheartedness to Jason. He was noticeably anxious about seeing the building in those dreams.

They traveled to Cape Coast in a taxi spewing blackened diesel emissions and a very friendly driver who answered as many of Callie's questions as he could. When the taxi approached *El Mina*, the first stop of the tour, the sight of the building off in the distance numbed Jason.

He had seen *El Mina* in dreams and learned much about it since, but seeing it in person gripped him in ways he had not expected. It stood tall and off-white, still dominating a much fuller landscape than that of the dreams. It was indeed right on the ocean, looking ominous and foreboding even in these modern times.

In antiquity, with people going in and never to be seen again, it must have been one terrifying place for the locals.

Upon entering the main structure of *El Mina*, Callie's cavalier attitude began to change. A strange ancestral presence could be felt as a more somber mood prevailed. Their tour group included many Europeans but no European-Americans. They walked through the main building first, touring the Governor's quarters and the chapel before entering the outside courtyard within the tall perimeter wall.

Jason froze. The obtuse angled abutment stood exactly as he had seen it in the dream.

The tour group was led to the rear, where the wall that still housed canons, though rusted and crumbling, sat aside a beautiful ocean view. Ghanaians busied themselves fishing and swimming in the waters to both sides of the castle's rocky base, knowledgeable but not mentally crippled by the horrors committed in this building in centuries gone by.

When they stepped into the male dungeon and saw the filth on the walls and floor, the playfulness of Callie's attitude was long gone. As the guide described the conditions that were endured by hundreds of thousands of Africans processed through this dungeon, a silence fell over the group.

The stench was still strong, hovering in the dungeon like a misty fog reflecting the misery captured and contained here by centuries of brutality. The tour guide said UNESCO had forbidden them from cleaning or altering the walls and floor.

The final stop was the female dungeon on the other side of the compound. Callie's face contorted after hearing the tour guide state this place was different from the male dungeon because along with urine and feces was the added reek of the menstrual.

Some of the people on the tour were overcome with emotion and tears flowed down solemn faces as the historical realities of the dungeon sunk in. Callie started to weep and Jason wrapped his arm around her shoulder, pulling her close. He escorted his pregnant wife out of the unspeakable dungeon.

Jason however, did not cry; he had already shed his tears... for him this was *déjà vu*.

The End

Elephants in Kenya by Janice Mazzallo 2018

IN EVERLASTING MEMORY

OF THE ANGUISH OF OUR ANCESTORS

MAY THOSE WHO DIED REST IN PEACE

MAY THOSE WHO RETURN FIND THEIR ROOTS

MAY HUMANITY NEVER AGAIN PERPETRATE

SUCH INJUSTICE AGAINST HUMANITY

WE, THE LIVING, VOW TO UPHOLD THIS.

Remembrance Signage at El Mina by Janice Mazzallo 2018

FOREVER AGO

Never fear the water.

It welcomed us
in our chains
when we had no names.
Promised to send
the goodbyes we never
said to you
in the dirges the waves
sing.

Place them in the stories
they forget to tell you.

That is where we died
that is where we wish to
live.

Hakeem Adam

Mealtime for Lion in Kenya by Janice Mazzallo 2018